# THEIR WORLD IN OURS

by M.C. Fiala

RoseDog Books
PITTSBURGH, PENNSYLVANIA 15238

RoseDog Books
585 Alpha Drive
Suite 103
Pittsburgh, PA 15238
Visit our website at www.rosedogbookstore.com

ISBN: 979-8-88729-046-1
eISBN: 979-8-88729-546-6

# Their World in Ours

# Dedication

*To my family, thank you for your support and encouragement.*

# CHAPTER 1
## THE EMPATH

My curse, or so I thought, started at birth with me very unaware. I am Aubrey McHale and was an unexpected baby that came five years after the birth of my sister, Lela. My sister was a witch, a strong witch, which was quite surprising considering that our mother was rather weak in her craft. Unfortunately for my sister, she had been cursed, so to speak, by our very own parents. My father, a shifter, and my mother, the witch (and a few other words that rhymed), were not really fit to breed and not interested in the family life. In order to maintain their lifestyle as it was, my parents sold my sister to the evil Medea, who was a princess of Hecate in the Underworld, for a large sum of money. Once Lela's training was complete at age fifteen, the trade would be made. Until then, my parents kept this information unbeknownst to either of us.

I, on the other hand, was born with a different kind of gift. My grandmother had been one of the greatest Empaths known to our world and I apparently carried that gene in addition to the weakened craft that existed in my mother. I was kind of a mutated version of old genetics. I had dirty blond hair that came down to my waist. I had a high metabolism so I pretty much ate whatever I wanted. Because of my empathic abilities, I was so sensitive to the world around me that we had to move further out of the city not long after I was born.

Even though there was a five-year difference between Lela and me, we were remarkably close from day one. By the time I reached two and a half years old, I was impossible to handle because of the sensations and emotions I felt coming in from the outside world. Lela became very protective of me since my mother could not be bothered with the whole matter. When I was sent away to live with my grandmother to learn to block out the world, my sister and I held each other, tears streaming down our faces.

I spent the next three years learning to mind block all the "feelings" coming in. My grandmother taught me to filter out each emotion so I could focus on what I needed. She had so expertly achieved this herself after a century of working with the Overseers that she now lived in peaceful ignorance of the outside world. The Overseers were a group of the strongest and highest Sorcerers, witches and warlocks that kept order among the paranormal beings on this planet and this dimension.

Nana, as I liked to call her, lived in a large log cabin deep in the woods in the Ozark National Forest which was well hidden by any campers or hikers. Her cabin contained three large rooms offset from the kitchen and living area. One of those rooms had been set up so she could play with her potions which had recently became her new hobby and she encouraged me to join her in the development of new potions.

The forest was rich with ingredients and her research often led her away for days. I never worried as I could always feel her presence in some form or fashion. I would know to not expect her to return as I watched her pile up her silver hair into a bun and pack a great deal of empty bags and a few concoctions she used for her survival against anything that may threaten her return.

She would lean in to peck me on the cheek, "Don't forget to practice the controls I've taught you and by all means, stay away from my potions until my return." I was too curious for my own good and had gotten into a bit a mischief in that room, but Nana would return and recover for me.

"I won't." I lied and she let out a little chuckle knowing better to believe I would stay away from her potions. I was just too curious. "How long do you think you will be gone this time?" I always asked this question so I knew when to reach out to her if I no longer felt her presence.

Her response was always the same, "Only a couple of days." She would give me the look and that was the end of my questions. My grandmother was not one to mince words when she could get her point across by a simple look in her eyes.

As my abilities strengthened, it also allowed me to sense my sister's emotions even though she was miles away. When she was sad, I would immediately call her and we would talk, mostly giggle over stories of mom and dad, for hours. I would tell her about the potions I had learned to create, and Lela would tell me about her latest spells.

By the time I returned home at the age of five, my father had built a large and modern house deep in the woods secluded from any neighbors. To access the house, one had to travel off the main roads and onto gravel roads. The gravel roads in our area were quite extensive and never-ending. It was easy to get lost just on the outskirts of the Lonesboro city limits.

The seclusion was of great benefit to me. I never had to worry about anyone coming around and looking in the multitudes of windows that surrounded the entire house. Every room, except for the closets, was surrounded by windows and visible from the woods outside. There were four bedrooms, a living room, den, a large kitchen with a dinette area, and a large laundry room that led to an immense library. Yes, we had a laundry room because my mother didn't have the talent to magically clean anything. The house contained a double-car garage which was only half occupied by my father's beloved Maserati and the other half contained weight training equipment with which my father was obsessed.

I spent much of my time in the closets on unbelievably bad days. Those were the days when the carnivorous forest animals were out feeding in full force and, although I could block the suffering the prey emitted, I still knew what was happening. I did not like it one bit…not one bit at all. Even after I learned to block, my mood would reflect what I was feeling. My mood would change from pain and suffering to happiness or to pure bitch in under a hundredth of a second, a change which occurred quite often.

Lela was always at my side during the difficult times and knew to keep her distance when I was just a bitch to be around. When I would get angry because of the inner turmoil, one too many lines were crossed, and I would become very destructive. Messes were made, things were broken, and injuries were had. My sister was really the only one who could calm me down. It took me years to fully learn how to block out the world around me.

Lela and I looked very much alike with our long dirty blond hair and more petite body than most at age of ten and five, respectively. We eventually developed an uncanny ability to communicate with each other with only our thoughts. We weren't sure if it was her witchcraft or my empathic abilities, but it was a life saver for me. Things became so much easier for both of us, especially for Lela to understand my pain and suffering. When I was having trouble blocking something troublesome late at night, I would metaphysically call out to Lela and she would leave her room to come and comfort me.

We became so good at communicating that we could make fun of our parents and make jokes about them at the dinner table while avoiding reprimand. Many times, we would start laughing at their expense which would eventually lead to our parents laughing with us, unknowingly, which only made us laugh harder. Of course, a few meals were left unfinished during these outbursts of laughter that led to tears.

Life was good during the last five years I had with my sister. I developed a knack for potions while she practiced her training as a witch. Things went on as usual until my sister turned fifteen. Then, suddenly, she was taken away, kicking and screaming, by a stranger that claimed that it was for her own good.

The woman called herself Medea. She was a tall and lanky lady, red hair, and appeared older but without any wrinkles to really define her age. What she wore I wouldn't call clothes. It was more like a negligee. Her arms and legs were thin and her skin was very dark, almost a blackish-blue.

In my opinion, she looked like a freak, and I could feel the evil that radiated from her body, her mind. The feeling was strong and a little painful. I couldn't imagine what she would have felt like to me if I hadn't been able to block her. It sent chills down my spine. I knew this was a very bad person.

Now at age 10, I didn't really understand what was going on and screamed to let my sister stay. Well, that didn't happen, and I couldn't fathom how my parents could allow such an act of cruelty. That was a powerfully sad day for me because I lost all contact with Lela after that. It left me with so much anger that I began to isolate myself in my bedroom closet avoiding my parents at all costs. What would they do to me, I used to wonder?

Not long after that, my parents suddenly announced that they were taking a trip and "would be back before I knew it". I was instructed to call my grandmother in case of an emergency, and they filled the kitchen with plenty of food and other amenities and were on their way.

After several months of being home alone, I received a visit from the local state police stating that my parents had disappeared in a boating accident. Apparently, they had been caught in a storm and their boat capsized. They were believed dead, or so I was told, and their bodies were never recovered.

I called my grandmother to tell her, and she explained to the police that she would come and stay with me. That never happened. She and I agreed that I was ready to be on my own and I had everything I could need in that house, so I remained alone for quite a while.

During my time alone, I practiced my potions from a book that my grandmother had given to me. Since the woods were thick around the house, I had access to a wide variety of plants, insects, fungi, and other possible potion-making materials. The house contained so many empty closets that I was able to fill multitudes of shelves with mostly innocent potions with temporary effects ready to sell to the human population.

I made some income for any additional essentials I needed by selling my potions. Being alone to play with my hobby/craft of potions, I spent almost every effort to avoid the outside world by developing my own website for those who bought these sorts of potions to stock in their shops. I would get the orders online, package them, and leave the boxes outside the front door for the local postal service to pick up. I was paid by credit card. It took a while to set up the site, but I learned quickly how to use the Internet to my advantage.

The potions I created for the human populace had to be carefully refined. There needed to be minimal residual mental side effects and no apparent physical side effects whatsoever and yet still offer just enough pizzazz that buyers kept coming back for more. My customers, mostly shop owners, loved the profits my potions brought them. Typical love potions, popularity potions and vengeance potions were mostly in the mind of the beholder of said potion, part real and part placebo effect. Really, it was up to my customers to convince their buyers of how effective the potions could be, make them see what they wanted to see.

I also had to make sure my potions didn't have any drug-induced side effects. Last thing I needed was to lose my license, which I received at age fourteen, due to black market potions. I had created a few medicinal potions for myself, mostly to calm my nerves when I felt something evil come across my empathic radar. I also got very good at many advanced potion spells and no one wanted me to go off halfcocked with my potion knowledge.

Unfortunately, the drug induced potions were high in demand on the black market and I had already been approached on several occasions with offers to develop and sell these recipes. After that, I started to concern myself with the safekeeping of my powerful potions that I would learn to develop.

I was accepted into Witchery University at age sixteen. I was excited about going to the University in Bum-Fucked Egypt, a couple of towns over from Lonesboro, to expand my skills. Being able to create potions of value for the supernatural world, to which I belonged, was an entirely different ballgame than what I had been able to do in the past. I had a long way to go before I learned those techniques extensively. Fortunately, I had always excelled at chemistry, math and imagination which I believed to be the basics for a profitable business of potions for both human-kind and the supernatural population.

CHAPTER 2

## EMPATH: THE BEGINNING

IN THE SMALL TOWNS OF ARKANSAS, MOST OF THE SUPER-natural kept to themselves and many of those families remained together, siblings avoiding life on their own. Most of the covens in the area were void of familiars as it was unnecessary.

Although I wasn't a purebred witch, I had received two familiars, Sushi and Sasha, about a year before I was to attend the University. I am not sure I was deserving of one, much less two, familiars but the forces of our world decided differently. They landed on my front doorstep and when I opened the door to inspect the noise, both walked past me into the house and made themselves at home. Each of them had their own abilities even though they were sisters, much like me and my sibling sister. Both were shape-shifters, although, I had never witnessed Sushi shift into anything or anyone. Between my two prissy-cat familiars and myself, there was a lot of bickering until we got acclimated to one another. We had the summer, before school started, to fall into a semi-routine.

Sushi was quite the "spazmanian" devil, as I liked to call her, and there were times that I had to mentally "tether" her from climbing the walls. I knew she was only playing but it still made it difficult to concentrate on what I was currently doing or sometimes to even sleep at night. Those nights I would empathically throw a shoe at her and that would calm her right down. As a solid black cat, Sushi was also very good at hiding. She was like the Cheshire cat, but I could only see the dim light reflect off her eyes and when she smiled, the corner of her eyes turned eerily upward. When there was no moon outside, when you could feel the darkness, and I could not sense her exact location, Sushi would quietly leap into my path and trip me up just for kicks, not that I needed any assistance from her since I was already the clumsiest person I knew. I would hear a brief giggle from her as she ran off, leaving me lying on the floor.

Sasha was amazing. She could and would change her appearance quite often to be whatever she wanted; a person, different animal, or even something as inert as a desk, albeit a slightly furry desk. To say the least, I was startled a few times before I realized her abilities. For instance, the late-night run in with a Cyclops in my own home. It had been a long day at school, so I stopped for some good ole southern fried catfish, which all three of us loved. My hands were full of books and dinner and I sensed nothing nearby. Sasha, the cyclops, opened the door and smiled. I screamed and food and books went flying everywhere. She laughed and….oh, so **not** funny! She immediately transformed back to what I believed was her true form, a black and white tuxedo cat, right before I could spiral into an anxiety attack. Even though her ability had been a lifesaver for me on many occasions, protecting me by appearing to be a very large and muscular male, she still had a mean streak much like her sister, Sushi.

•    •    •

After I was accepted into Witchery U, Sushi and Sasha and I
had a debate about whether they would attend the University
with me. I didn't think it would be a good idea, but they thought
I would be less anxious with them at my side. We finally agreed
that I would try it by myself first and they could come along if I
had difficulty adjusting. I was so excited to learn about bigger and
better potions that I had forgotten about the people, so many
people of various ages from early puberty to young adults. And,
they had feelings. Lots of them. I was so ready for school and I
wanted to get out of my rut and out of Lonesboro; what I was not
prepared for were paranormal beings, lots of them and of all
kinds. The only real exposure to people was that that I had with
my family. Now that they had been gone for several years, I was
used to the isolation and solitude. Everything I had needed had
been delivered to the house. Also, what I was not prepared for, as
I had hoped, were the people's immense emotions flowing like a
waterfall over my head. I was so overwhelmed when I first set
foot on campus that I almost turned around and headed home.
But I focused on blocking and pushed through it. To say the least,
the girls came with me the next day.

I didn't attempt to fly unlike most of the others who had con-
quered that ability at a young age. So, I stood out like a sore
thumb. The first day on campus, there were a LOT of young and
old flying from here to there. I never learned to fly but I could
levitate. Whatever it took to move in any direction, I didn't have
it. I could "swim" through the air, but I looked funny since it was-

n't very effective. No one else seemed to need any help flying. It was quite discouraging. So, I spent my time on the ground and the few friends I developed were okay with that.

I sensed different specialties in each person and had so much anxiety that I had to keep up my shields. I felt so small coming from a people of one during my teen years. Since I had no introduction to college from an older sibling, as it should have been, I had a lot of trouble adjusting. Sasha and Sushi spent much of their time protecting me from bad influences except one and I have no idea why they took to her so easily. Martha was her name and fighting was her game. She was a good witch but played a mean game. Somehow, from opposite ends of the spectrum, we became attached at the hip upon first meeting in one of our classes. It hit me hard when I heard a voice inside my head make a sarcastic remark about the current instructor. "He has got to be a thousand years old, I bet he has dementia." I could block just about any average witch and Martha still got into my head so it caught me off guard. I muffled a laugh and turned to her as she turned to me and we just smiled at each other. We could project thoughts to each other with no effort. It was weird to have someone else inside my head besides my sister and I immediate let her know to tread lightly. Crazy as she was, we became good friends against all odds. Martha had no care in the world and was always either in cahoots with me, playing pranks on others or we were playing magical jokes on each other. The pranks came easy since we were so different; we didn't know what to expect from the other. She was mean in her pranks (did I mention that she had a mean streak?) but we both took it in fun and was entertaining to others unless they were on the receiving end of the joke.

My potions training became more focused and, with the addition to an increased ability to my witchcraft, I learned how to develop my potions and spells to take on a life of their own. One of the first of these potions I made at home specifically for dear Mad Martha, as I liked to call her. It was better than the one that turned her urine blue and literally freaked her out over it until I told her it was my doing. It was a harmless potion, short term and very funny. From that point on, it was "on" between the two of us. Her jokes were a bit more painful. She would jump me during a party, laughing all the while, and the crowd would spread, trying to avoid getting caught up in Mad Martha's fun fury of pain. She usually would get the better of me in hand-to-hand combat but occasionally, I would come out on top. So, after her latest attempt to best me in a crowd, I threw my latest home brew at her with a yell of a spell in the middle of a crowded cafeteria.

She looked up at me and said, "What have you done to me now?"

I just smiled and shrugged "You have something in your hair".

She reached up and her hand came down with a pile of her wild hair in it. "I can't believe you did this. You're getting better" and she just laughed. By the time we got back to her dorm room, she was completely bald. She walked to the mirror and fell on the floor laughing. "For your sake, I sure hope you know how to reverse this", she managed to say in between her cackles.

"No can do." I was laughing so hard I could barely breathe. "This one is going to have to run its course. It should be back to normal by morning." She turned to me and gave me an evil look and I quit laughing. I knew I was going to pay dearly for this one at some point, but it was worth it. I couldn't hold back with my laughter any longer, let out a loud laugh and curled over, holding my stomach. The initial shock she had felt when she looked into the mirror was a rare sight for me and I was ecstatic that I got the better of her. After a while, the laughing subsided and like that, it was over, until next time.

•     •     •

The "footprint" potion was one of my personal creations that I was quite proud of as it could mislead anyone who tried to back-track the potion to the witch who created the potion. This solution became a base for all my potions to keep more trouble away from me at the University. Only a very strong witch or warlock could recognize the potion for what it was. I was fortunate to not have been caught by the Headmaster of the University.

Martha was always full of adventure. Our weekends were kicked off at dinner and then continued nonstop at my house for the remainder of the weekend. Her witchcraft was so much stronger than mine and she managed to hide the location of my home from whomever tagged along; and I always knew she would have my back until the following Monday. I look back at those early years at the University and wonder how I managed to excel at anything.

Martha was always willing to be my guinea pig for any new potions I whipped up at home, so we were a good fit and, eventually, pretty good friends. She also taught me some "tricks of the trade" to learning some of the more difficult lessons.

Once everyone heard about our little pranks, they laughed along at my latest attack on Martha but were very cautious not to fall victim to our pranks. When Martha and I were together, I seemed to have more control on my empathic abilities. My internal walls were always up but it was easier around Martha. I didn't seem to have the fear of being side-swiped of some intense emotion and I never knew whether it was of Martha's doing or not.

On Fridays, for entertainment, I would get Martha to try out my latest potion unknowing anything about its purpose. Those potions had been developed specifically with Martha in mind and had no other purpose but to mess with her. There was the time when she stood up to leave the dinner hall only to find that she had grown a large white fluffy tail. She had more fun with that prank than I got out of it. She could have just zapped it away but no. She held it high as we walked out of the hall and across campus to her dorm. She loved the attention and was always game for anything at any time. The woman was not scared of anything. Our relationship was like we fed on each other through pain, suffering and lots of laughter.

During the first couple of years at the University, certain potions had their advantages since I could go out carousing with my "friends" (and I use that word loosely) nonstop. When they became staggering idiots off the moonshine we consumed, I would always appear perfectly sober when, in reality, I was as drunk as a skunk on the inside. I was always the happiest drunk in the crowd, numbing the nerves to any outside (negative) sensations. I liked to play impractical jokes on the others which kept everyone's spirits high and kept everyone from getting into trouble. I guess you could say that I was the responsible drunk out of the group if there were such a thing.

•  •  •

That is what I liked about potions. No one really bothered with potions anymore since they could hone their own magic to be faster, more reliable, and stronger. Even though I didn't have the ability to be a strong witch, I had created some very strong and dangerous potion spells which could take effect long after I was not around. And, if no one was around, they weren't prepared to defend themselves with their own magic.

# CHAPTER 3
## THE PLAN

FROM THE BEGINNING OF OUR FRIENDSHIP CAME STRONG trust and understanding with Martha. Granted, she would always retaliate when she was the butt of my potions, but I expected no less from her. Her aggressiveness helped me to be a stronger and quicker witch. We settled down after a time as both our studies became more time consuming.

Over the last year at the University, we spent a lot of time talking about the past and the future and I eventually told her the story of my sister's fate. "There are a lot of things that you don't know about me, Martha. I probably should have told you all of this sooner but it is pretty painful for me." I paused to see if she was really listening to me and not distracted by her own thoughts. I knew I couldn't repeat myself once I got it out. I had spent so many years trying to avoid thoughts of my sister, literally trying to forget her. I had already watched Nana pass over and my sister, as far as I knew, was all that was left of my younger life, if she was still alive.

"Martha, look at me." Her eyes finally focused on mine and I knew I had her attention. "I have, or I should say I had a sister. She was older than me by five years and my parents sold her off to some evil witch from the Underworld. It has been almost ten years since I last saw her."

Martha's eyes widened. I guess she was a little surprised that I had not revealed this to her earlier on. "I am so sorry. Why didn't you tell me?"

"I was just trying to move on with my life, trying to forget the past. That's why I was so crazy when we first met. I was trying not to spiral downwards. Everyone else seem to come from a normal home life."

"What was her name?" She asked as if she believed that she was no longer alive.

"Lela. We were close as children." Martha didn't interrupt so I kept on. "It was on her 15th birthday that she had achieved enough power that it was time for her to go away, according to my parents. I learned later from my grandmother that it was the evil doings of my very own parents." I took a deep breath and exhaled. Martha remained quiet. "I was so angry for years after that but being alone forced me to focus on survival. I just couldn't understand how my parents could do such a thing and only because of their love of fortunes." I had not shed one tear while I released the pain and tension of that day that had plagued me all those years ago.

Martha was shocked. "How could a parent do something like that to their own child?"

Sadly, I replied, "I don't know why they even had children. They sent me away to live with my grandmother when I was very young because they didn't want to put in the effort to guide me through my empathic sensitivities."

"Was your grandmother an empath?" Martha asked curiously.

"Yes," I answered. "And apparently, my sister and I were both mistakes. I don't think they wanted children at all."

"And your sister, was she an empath as well?" Martha asked.

"No, she was a strong witch. I think that was her appeal to the demon world." I responded.

"I wish you told all of this to me sooner. I could have at least been there for you if you had needed to talk." Martha was trying not to be angry with me, keeping something so major from her over the years while at the University. She had known I was alone with only my grandmother to fall back on and she didn't ask a lot of questions or pry about my personal life. She was funny that way. I had played my personal past so close to the vest or it would have broken me. Of course, she hadn't talked much about her past either so I guess we were even.

"I wish there was some way I could find her, to bring her back from the evil, if she is even still alive." I didn't want to ask Martha for her help, but she was all I had, and I knew I couldn't do it alone.

Martha began asking a lot of questions about the evil woman who took Lela. She asked about her name, her looks, how her voice sounded. "Do you know the name of the demon who took her away?"

"Actually, I do. Her name was Medea. She was an evil looking being and I could feel her power as soon as she appeared." I thought back on that horrible day. "My sister didn't have a chance against her."

Martha reacted when I said the demon's name. "I have heard of her. She is well known in the Underworld for her relentless need of more power. She feeds on the powers of others. One of my professors warned us of her when dealing with demons."

"What do you mean 'dealing with demons? Is that what you intend do with your life?" Even though Martha and I had known each other for years, we really hadn't talked much about our own schooling, so I knew very little about what her strengths were. We had spent way too much time having fun, and, I realized, that she had been the one saving grace throughout my education. She had kept me on my toes.

She laughed. "Are you serious? You really don't know what I study?"

"Well, I suspected your power was battle tested but not why." I smiled sheepishly. "Guess we haven't really talked like this in the past. Pretty weird, huh?"

"Yeah, I guess we haven't talked much about anything but spells and potions and people, but not each other." She sounded solemn. She realized that we really didn't know each other as well as it appeared by most. But, I knew that our trust in each other was strong. I knew I could always count on her.

And she proved so when she spoke again. "I can help find your sister. I can't guarantee we can get her back, but I would be glad to help you try." She was calm when she said, " I know things. Evil things, evil beings and much about the Underworld." Her voice softened as if telling me would cause harm. "We had to learn about the evil in order to beat it. It hasn't been easy these last couple of years."

"Why didn't you say anything?" I asked. "I could have been there for you as well." She had hidden it well as I never felt anything negative from her. She kept it close to the chest like I had done with my past.

"Oh, but you were," she replied. "If it had not been for you and your antics, I couldn't have handled the stress." We just sat in silence reflecting over the last several years.

After I finished all the details of the story of my sister and how she was so abruptly taken away, I asked Martha, "Do you really think you could help me find and rescue Lela?"

Martha began to explain to me about the nature of evil. "One thing you always have to remember when dealing with evil, know your strengths and limitations, and most of all, remember yourself. It's easy to get lost in the madness that is evil." My brow rose but I didn't speak. "There are different kinds of evil as well. There is the physical, mental, emotional and the magical affect. The physical is easy to overcome if you know what you're doing. But the mental and magical are totally a different fight. Their magic can make it difficult to see reality from truth. The emotional effect I don't think you should have a problem with being an Empath. You can block that type of threat and probably minor mental affects but demons are a tricky bunch. You must know what is right and follow your gut, not what you think you see or hear….and with it is a strong sensation that evil can attack. It can be so simple or very complex. You, as an empath, could sense the difference if you are trained so. I can help you, but it will take time and we will have to begin with your understanding of the evil that lurks in the Underworld. One of my professors has first-hand experience and he has taught me well. Do you really think you are up for this?"

"Honestly, I have thought about this for a long time. I'm not as angry as I used to be, but I feel responsible somehow that my sister was taken. Maybe if I hadn't been born, our parents wouldn't have been as likely to give her up. Maybe it wouldn't have mattered. They were pretty selfish."

I sat in thought for a minute until Martha interrupted my thoughts. "I can understand that, but you need to know what you are getting yourself into."

I looked up at her, "No, I am not sure if I am up for this", I said addressing her previous question. "I just know that I have to at least try. Lela needs to know that she is wanted and loved. I can't just let this be."

Martha got that grin on her face, the one she gets when we are fighting for fun. "Okay, then. We better start training. Can we do this at your house? We'll need some privacy. I don't want anyone to get word of this. This is not a task for a youngling like yourself and, if the professors get wind of this, we will be restricted from doing the research that needs to be done."

I nodded. "We also have our familiars." Martha's strong personality invited a strong familiar, a Nemean lion and appropriately named Neme (pronounced enema). Although he was a powerful beast, he took to my familiars unreasonably so. He was more protective of Sushi and Sasha almost as much as I was. It was quite a site to see this immortal lion take to my two small cats although they were strong in their own rights.

Martha started her research on the demon that took Lela and we began to put together a plan. The most difficult part of the trip would be finding Lela's location. Lela could have been sold ten times over according to Martha. We would have to travel the same path she had if she is no longer under Medea's possession.

While Martha was doing her research, I spent some time with Sushi and Sasha, explaining that we were planning a trip to the Underworld. Sushi sat quietly, as if this would be a piece of cake. Sasha was a little more realistic with a bit of reluctance to venture into the darkness. I took Sasha aside later and asked her about Sushi's reaction (or nonreaction, as the case may be) to all of this.

Sasha responded, "There is a reason that Sushi does not shift. It can be very painful for her because she is cursed to shift into a monster. Granted, it will be of benefit to you and she will recover but it won't be easy on her."

"Well, let's hope that it never comes to that." I said trying to damper the worried look in Sasha's eyes.

Sasha straightened up and replied, "But you can help her control some of the emotions along with it. If you could learn to extend your blocking as you do for your own emotions, it would diminish the turmoil brought on by the form she takes."

"And just how do I learn to do that?"

"When she shifts, you will have to lower your own shields to find her inner turmoil, then, mentally, bring them back up with her inside. It will take some practice but she can show you how. She has had some experience with this."

I didn't ask any more questions but turned to Sushi. She simply nodded her head once and then turned and walked away. We started working on blocking her emotions when she shifted the next morning.

●　　　●　　　●

Martha's research led her to a contact, Micca who was warlock at the University and had much more experience dealing with the entities of the Underworld. He indicated that in order to get the information we needed, we would have to acquire something to barter. Martha and I decided that once we finished our schooling, which was just around the corner, we would spend our times gathering financial strength. Martha took a job way out west and I stayed right where I was, working on and selling my potions. Even though I was financially secure thanks to my grandmother, Martha still needed to build up some contacts.

We would reach out to each other from time to time, updating each other on our status and any information our research had revealed. We didn't see each other for several months but she had indicated that she had found someone that may be able to help. We were getting close to making our move.

Using a map that Martha had sent, I had mapped out the locations Martha had indicated to me and attempted to follow Lela's path through sensation. The first time I touched the map that Martha gave me made my fingertips tingle. I was not sure why but assumed it was the map itself that had magical powers. After a while, I found that when I traced my fingers along a wrong path, the tingling would subside. I felt a whisp of a cool breeze and heard my grandmother's voice, "Follow the path you can feel." And then there was silence. I knew then that my grandmother was helping me from the other side. As I worked, I listened for her again but heard nothing until my fingers moved on a wrong road on the map. I would feel the whisp of wind again and would move my hands back to the fork in the road where I had lost the feeling. The map that Martha gave me had its own magic powers and I knew then that the tingling was the sense of my sister. Now, being so familiar to magical things, it didn't take long for me to figure this out and find the most recent location of my sister. Once I was ready, I reached out to Martha to let her know that I had located the last area in which she had been kept. Martha needed to gather her small army of three fellow demon fighters and then explained the mission and came up with a final plan. I waited to hear from her for further instructions. I knew it wouldn't be long now.

## CHAPTER 4
### *THE SORCEROR*

**M**EANWHILE, THOUSANDS OF MILES AWAY, MAXIMILLIAN
Ferric walked through his new home, rooms illuminating
as he entered. Max could not believe he had been given this opportunity, even more so, the responsibility. The Overseers had
originally thought he was too weak but he had always been a cautious man. He was a bit introverted and had a gentle personality
but he was smart and he was powerful. His 5' 8" height and boyish good looks kept him in good relations with most but left questions for the Overseers as to his power. Max's dirty-blond hair fell
gently below his shoulders and was streaked with gentle white
streaks that outlined his face. His boyish face included a small
dimple in his chin and thick luscious lips. His blue eyes were set
deep and when he would look up, you could see the strength of
his sorcery in them, that was the only sign of his power. He often
had been underestimated. He could be as ruthless and as evil as
those in the Underworld. Max had fought hard to keep the evil
at bay from his watch at the University in the British Isle. He still
hadn't made it easy for the Overseers to make their decision about
this.

When he faced Hermes in a battle to release those witches still living on the earth and had been bartered from their families, it was then that he had to reflect on the prophecy that had been foretold at birth. He decided that it was time to focus on his training and face the prophecy that was his future. He was meant to protect. Once he was promoted to his new position, he knew he could no longer show any weakness. Once his reputation as a strong sorcerer reached the Underworld, the Overseers decided that Max would measure up to the prophecy.

As he continued to climb the stairs to the tower of his new home, which stood high above the surrounding rainforest, he knew it would be hard to protect his new home and the species that had come to live there. The isolated island of Fatimia in the fourth dimension of the Mediterranean was not visible to the human or any magical eye, and its inhabitants would now and always be his top priority. There was a lot of forces that played upon this small island and Max knew that his responsibilities to the people living below him was critical and his commitment to them would not falter until his death. Reaching the top of his new residence, he turned slowly, looking out upon the deep blue waters that surrounded the island. Initially, he had lived quietly among the paranormal community that lived on the outskirts of the western part of the island. He had to see for himself that the people that were brought over would maintain their cover and keep the secret that lay deep inland, in the rain forest that covered the mountain. Now, as he looked at the endless turquois and blue waters, he knew that his patience and belief in the Overseers paid off.

*This feels right*, he thought. *Now I have only one thing left to do, and the island will be as it should be, recovering from the damage done* *by my predecessor who had been killed prior to the Shift. And **she** should be ready by now. This will be a good move for her after being isolated and alone all these years. Question is, can I convince her to come? She would no longer be able to maintain her emotional distance from others and it would be difficult.*

•     •     •

Max Ferric had been watching Aubrey McHale from afar since she was born. He had watched her suffering, watched her growth and her training. He was sure she was the one that would be able to communicate and help with this new species. She could quite possibly help them understand the dangers that they would face if exposed to not only the Underworld but even humans. After watching her from a distance all these years, silently, he had become infatuated with the very young Empath. Making contact needed to be subtle and unobtrusive and he had to keep his feelings always hidden. If she got any sense of his feelings for her, it could destroy the safety of the island and the power it took to keep the Underworld from discovering the new species that had recently been relocated here. After her training in the healing powers, she would be the perfect fit as the one of the healers on the island. Since not much was known about these ancient species from an entirely different galaxy than ours, an Empath/Healer would be the best source of medical attention should anything befall these creatures while under our watch.

•     •     •

Max had decided to make contact with Aubrey sooner rather than later. He knew she would be reluctant as her focus was on finding and returning her own sister back to her home in Arkansas. He would have to convince her that the priorities to educate her as a Healer for the Soluzari took precedent after locating her sister. She needed to be prepared to meet the Soluzari and began her education on all that is Soluzari.

CHAPTER 5
# THE SOLUZARI

THE SOLUZARI WAS THE NAME OF THE SPECIES INDICATED by the prophecy. Where they originated is still not quite understood but it had been destroyed along with many of their own kind. Only several hundred had escaped through their magic and into our galaxy and onto our planet. Their perspective of our galaxy and dimensions had to be quite different from theirs, at least that is what they had tried to explain, limited in their ability for verbal communication. They had entered our world and into our dimension, not far from the Great House that was home to the Overseers of all metaphysical/paranormal species here on earth. They, and according to the prophecy, radiated power of unprecedented proportions and because of that, the hundreds of Soluzari would be transported to an uninhabited dimension found through a rare and ancient portal in the northern and most desolate part of the British Isle. The location had been documented in an ancient prophecy by an unknown source to house hundreds of a new species. That is when the Overseers decided to investigate the portal, found it a viable location, an island in the fourth dimension of the Mediterranean, for a new colony to develop and live safely and privately until the prophecy had finally come to light and the new species to arrive.

The prophecy that had been documented a century before spoke of this alien race and the difficulties they were to face, when they entered our atmosphere. Their existence had been part of many discussions leading up to the decade in which they were prophesized to appear. Many of the Overseers were doubtful that they existed. Many believed that they could be a threat to our existence, both paranormal and human. The prophecy indicated that they were a delicate race and would require our protection.

The Soluzari arrived in small capsules that cluttered the pastures of Scotland, collected and transported to the Overseers where they were released from their pods. They turned out to be small and childlike creatures. Their maximum height was only a couple of feet and their arms and legs (two of each) were as thin as twigs but very flexible. Their bodies were about a couple of inches thicker and a bit darker color than their extremities. For the most part, they were bluish-green in color with a translucent appearance with very similar features as a human. Their hair color varied among them. They also had catlike facial features. They slept upright as if standing very still although if you looked close enough, you could see that their tiny feet were not touching the ground. It was a very peaceful sight.

They yielded much power but rarely exerted their abilities within their species as it was not necessary. Their innocence and kindness maintained a balance within their race that such power was unnecessary. But fallen into the wrong hands, as the evil that lurked within and on our own planet, could cause the shift in balance between good and evil in unprecedented proportions.

Therein lies the responsibility of the Overseers to maintain the privacy of their arrival and existence in our world.

Max was the Sorcerer that would inhabit the island with selected paranormal influences with high values and standards. Upon the arrival and until the new species had a chance to adapt to our paranormal world, they would remain in secrecy and kept away from any evil, and even more so, humans (who could be as evil as those that roamed in Hell). So, preparations had begun to prepare for the relocation of this new species. The Overseers did not know how much time that they had but they knew they only had months to prepare before the Shift to their new location. The Overseers could only protect their existence in this dimension for a short time before word would likely get out. Fortunately, the majority of the Overseers believed in the prophecy and began populating and developing the island two years prior to the arrival of the Soluzari.

# Chapter 6
## Aubrey and the Sorcerer

As I finished packing up another shipment of potions to be picked up outside my front door, I felt something stir deep inside. It was not a familiar presence. As I walked to the front door with the package, the feelings of something powerful got stronger. I opened my mind and felt a rush of emotions. It was coming from just outside my front door. I stood very still, sending signals out to Sushi and Sasha for protection. Both appeared as two large cats, Sasha, an oversized lioness and Sushi, a manticore which even scared me a little. They sat down at my sides both exceeding my own height of 5'4". Once I had determined that the threat was not evil, I slowly opened the door. There stood a man with the most intense blue eyes and a delicate face. He wore blue khaki pants and a white silk shirt covered with a light tan trench coat. The shirt was unbuttoned enough to show his muscled chest. It was like looking at the cover of a cheap romance novel but he was real and, of course, had more clothes on. When he spoke, his voice was deep but smooth.

"Good morning, Aubrey McHale." His voice sent chills down my spine and I felt as if I had known this man my entire life. "I don't mean to startle you as I am sure you are not used to having strangers approach your door. Although, I see you are well protected by your familiars." He commented as he glanced to each side of me. He didn't seem deterred in the least. "Please let me introduce myself. My name is Maximillian Ferric but you can call me Max. I am with the Overseers." Everyone knew who the Overseers were so I was a little shocked that someone of such power and respect approached me. He continued, "I have a proposition for you."

I opened my mind a little more and felt no threat from this stranger. "How do you know my name and how did you know to find me here?"

"I have been watching you for most of your life, Aubrey, and knew your grandmother very well. I offer my condolences on her passing. She passed over early in life but I think she was ready. We knew each other from the House of Elders in the British Isles. She was one of the greatest Empaths of her time. I had hoped we could have been introduced through her to make this easier on you but Fate had another idea."

My grandmother never had talked much about her past but I knew she had been wise and experienced way beyond her years. This was the first person I had ever met that knew of her and of her powers. I was both excited and leery. Had I not had Martha put a radar to detect evil on my property, I would not have invited him in. "You say you knew of my grandmother?" He nodded his head. "Would you like to come in?" His presence left me with a sense of peace, of safety and trust. That was rare for me. I never trusted a stranger much less an acquaintance. Martha had been the only one to earn my trust in my early adult life. And now, this man standing before me, propositioning me, seemed both normal and yet unusual. I decided I would hear what Max had to say before jumping to any conclusions about his sincerity and hold judgement until the end.

I set the box on the doorstep and waived him inside. I led him into the living room which was seldom used and always in immaculate condition. Sitting in a leather rocker/recliner, I pulled my legs into my lap comfortably. Sushi and Sasha, maintaining their current forms trotted over to sit on either side of me as a warning to the new intruder. I waved to the couch in front of me encouraging him to have a seat. Max settled in on the edge of the couch.

He cleared his throat before he began. "I will get right to the point. All I am about to tell you is for your ears only." He paused waiting for me to acknowledge what he had said.

"Well, since I know very few people, that will be easy enough." I responded half-heartedly.

"This is a serious proposition that will require your complete commitment, Aubrey."

"Okay, I'm listening." I straightened up and the grin went away from my face.

"I am a sorcerer and have been given the responsibility to fulfill a prophecy that has come into play. It is to protect an island and its habitants in the fourth dimension in the Mediterranean. Every witch, warlock, shifter and other paranormal species have been hand selected to come and live and work on this island. I have been waiting for you to complete your education before I brought my proposal before you. We are in much need of an Empath and you are the strongest one I know and can trust and I have searched far and wide. In addition, we need a Healer as well and the elders and I think it is in the best interest of this post that the Empath and the Healer are one in the same."

"Excuse me, Max, let me stop you right there. A Healer I am not. I am familiar with many healing potions but have never actively used them on anyone except myself. I am not sure I am the person you are looking for." I wanted to make that clear.

Max continued. "I am fully aware of what your healing capabilities are and that is why I would like to introduce you to one of the best healers I know to teach you the basics. It would be a crash course. The most important is of your Empathic abilities which I will eventually explain to you. But first and foremost, I must get your full commitment to your journey that has been prophesized and come to fruition just recently. We are under a lot of pressure to ensure that the right people are in place now that the Shift has been completed." Max decided that the less information he offered was for the best. He would explain it all once I arrived to Fatimia.

"Max, not to belittle what you have said here but you have spoken of much vagueness and it is difficult to understand what you are asking of me." I paused, thinking of my sister and my current plan to find her and bring her home. "I currently have another priority that is in its planning stages."

"Yes," he replied, "locating and saving your sister from the evil that was thrown upon her as a teenager. I can help with that but only if you will agree to continue your education over the next couple of months in the healing arts. I will offer all the help I can to you and your friend Martha in order to rescue your sister."

I thought long and hard what he was asking of me. I didn't question what he already knew about my agenda. I didn't mention the map or that I had already located my sister. He probably already knew anyway. The thought of having help in rescuing Lela could be a great benefit and prove to be more successful than with Martha, her small crew, and me alone. The tradeoff seemed fair enough.

"Just how do you know Martha?" His mention of her had surprised me, only a little. He did say he had been watching me over the years. Of course, he knew who Martha was.

"Aubrey, I am familiar with the more powerful people coming out of the Universities." Now that surprised me. It told me just how powerful Martha actually was.

Max continued. "It is my job to know what they are doing with their powers. Evil has a way of making it into the goodwill of many and the Overseers must know who to trust. Evil can hide in the best of many."

"But Martha fights Evil. I trust her more than anyone in my life." I thought about her chosen field and wondered if she could be persuaded to change her ways. I thought about our history in our earlier years at the University and how mischievous she had been. "Granted, she has a mean streak but isn't that what it takes to stand up to Evil?"

Max straightened up. "I have watched her closely as I do all of those in that chosen profession. She is as hard as they come and cannot be persuaded to cross over. That I am sure of." He sighed and said, "I would not offer my assistance if I thought she was of any threat."

"So, you will help us? Have you spoken with Martha about this?"

"Not yet but I will have someone reach out to her. But all of this is under one absolute condition. You cannot tell her about the Prophecy or your involvement with it or me. Is that understood?"

"I understand although I do not like keeping things from her."

"Oh, trust me dear. She has her hands full and will spend a lifetime fighting those that will come after her for trying to steal your sister away."

"What about me? Will I be in danger?"

"Yes, but, you and, hopefully, your sister will be well hidden by that time." Max stood. "Now I must go but I suggest you get your affairs in order as we will be expecting you to start your studies immediately. Now you need to go and rescue your sister. Should you need any help, please do not hesitate to send a signal to me." I raised my eyebrows to him to question how. He read my mind and immediately responded, "Oh, I will sense your urgency for help."

"How are you so sure she is still alive?" I was not sure of this myself even though I had the location when I last touched the map. I wanted to know how much he knew.

"She is too valuable to be destroyed. Once we locate her..."

I immediately interrupted him. "Oh, I have located her last living position on a map Martha gave to me. I am just not sure she is still alive. I cannot sense her mind."

"Well, things will be easier once you can free her from her shackles, she will be a strong force to reckon with." And with that, he headed towards the door. "Your instructions will follow shortly. I suggest you maintain this residence even after you have left." Meaning to not sell the house. "It was a pleasure to finally have met you in person, Aubrey McHale. Do not speak of this visit to anyone." And with that, he was gone.

I sighed with the thought of another project. All I wanted to focus on was my sister. But if this Sorcerer was willing to help, it would be worth it. It didn't hurt that he was easy on the eyes. I had never seen a man of such form and perfection. And the blue eyes were hypnotizing. For some reason, I felt a sense of obligation to this man. And being alienated (to some extent) among other paranormal people I had met at the University, it would be nice to find a new home and among people I could be myself. I knew of no one that possessed my abilities and made me feel a little isolated from the witches, warlocks and shifters. Besides my only friend, Martha, and her familiar, I felt as if I were a stranger in a strange land.

•   •   •

Max took a deep breath once he returned to the UK. It had been most difficult to hide his feelings for Aubrey. Maybe, he thought, someday I will tell her. In the meantime, he prepared a colleague for the meeting with Martha. She had to approach her carefully as Martha was a cautious soul. Since Martha was currently in the middle of a job, it could take a few days to get her to reunite with Aubrey. He had decided to send someone in his place thinking it best to keep his involvement with the rescue of Lela withheld from Martha. Aubrey's future and that of her sister's must remain hidden from everyone except the Overseers and those on the island.

•  •  •

By the time I cleaned up the lab and prepared for my journey with Martha, I was exhausted. The girls and I laid down for a short nap to wake with the sound of banging on the front door. I reached out with my senses and it was a very familiar feeling, lots of chaos and energy. I knew it had to be Martha. I opened my mind and said, "Martha?"

I heard her voice in my head. "Hey, it's me. Let me in."

I got up walked to the front room and opened the door to find Martha standing there with bags in hand. "Well, it's about time. I got word from some sorcerer that we needed to hurry if we were to retrieve Lela from the depths of hell. I am not sure what the hurry is but here I am."

I smiled. "Yes, you are and in all your glory." Martha was not a petite person to say the least. She was about 5'7" and was full figured. Her long wavy brown hair was dull but she made up for it by wearing bright red lipstick. Her eyelids were caked with shadow, bronze on the top and green on the lower eyelids. Her lashes were long even without the usual back mascara she wore. She wore tight fitting blue jeans with a loose maroon blouse flowing over her midsection and black leather boots that came up just below her knees.

Since I had been working most of the day I was still in my shorts and a tee shirt. I took a step back to let her in. I was a little surprised to see her so quickly as I had just spoken with Max. "I take it you spoke to Max?"

She raised her eyebrows and said, "Who?"

"I thought you said you spoke to a sorcerer. Who was this person?"

"It was no man that I spoke with. It was a woman who got word that if we were to retrieve Lela, it had to be now. She said she was from the land of the Overseers. She gave me no reason to question her."

Martha was a good judgment of character but I was surprised that Max had not met with her directly. I did not mention Max's name again as per his request. "I spoke with someone as well today and I was told the same thing." I turned and motioned to the map laying out on the dining room table. She followed me to the dining room where the large map of the Underworld was spread out. "I don't know where you found this map but it is amazing. I could actually sense Lela's presence as she moved in the Underworld."

Martha leaned over the map and Sasha and Sushi both came running up onto the table to greet Martha, both sliding across the map and almost landing on Martha. "Hey there girls. You have been taking good care of my friend I see." Martha turned to me. "Once I realized the powers of the map, I knew you would be the only one to sense what lays beyond the roads and mountains. No one else that I know has the powers to sense what lies beneath. That's why it was so easy to retrieve." She looked around. "Are you ready to leave in the morning? The others will be waiting at the entrance to meet up with us."

"I am. I just finished cleaning up the lab and packing some items we may need along the way." I did not mention my visit with the sorcerer, Max Ferric, although I wanted to. He was a handsome man and I found him very intriguing. As much as

I wanted to tell Martha about everything he had told me, I knew Max was right. I had to keep my future a secret, even from her.

C H A P T E R  *7*

## *T***RIP TO THE** *U***NDERWORLD**

**T**HE NEXT MORNING BEGAN EARLY. MARTHA AND THE girls had made coffee and breakfast by the time I had woken up at 6AM. I dressed in jeans and a t-shirt and headed to the kitchen. We ate in silence as everyone was a little apprehensive of what laid ahead. I, personally, was a nervous wreck. So many thoughts ran across my mind. What would the Underworld be like? Would it be a constant battle? What would we encounter along the way? Would Lela even still be alive? Would she recognize me?

I finally broke the silence. "Martha, I know you said there is an entrance to the Underworld not far from where I last sensed Lela. What can we expect to encounter upon entering?"

Both the girls and I watched Martha finish chewing and swallowing her last bite. She took a deep breath and began. "The tunnel we'll be entering is rarely used and we will likely be able to make it to the pathway that leads to Lela without incident....maybe. There are no guarantees what we will encounter along the way. It will also depend on if we can maintain our shields as we enter. Once we get to the pathway, it will be a bit more difficult to maintain our shields." She took another deep breath. "I have an idea of what we might encounter but the entourage we are meeting will have more experience with the Underworld than I do. My experience has been more involved fighting the demons that are here on our dimension."

Sasha was the first to ask about this entourage even though I had vaguely been briefed the day before. "Who are these people anyway? Sushi and I may have run into them in the past." Her last comment made me realize how little I knew of their past or that they had one at all. I didn't even know how old they were.

As Martha waved her hand over the table, the food bowls and our plates and silverware made their way to the kitchen counter and sink. I was amazed at how easy that was for her. Her magic had strengthened. "There is Stan Wohols, Eric Sedan, and Micca Rice. Aubrey, you may remember Micca from the University. He agreed to help us since classes are not in session."

Sasha pressed for more information. "I remember Micca and I have heard of Stan but not Eric. Is he a warlock as well?"

"Actually, Eric is a demon shifter. He is very similar to Sushi but he came by it naturally, not cursed. He is very strong and it takes a lot to even knock him down. He will come in handy if it comes to a physical fight just as will Sushi."

At Martha's comment, Sushi jumped down from her chair and walked away. I don't think she was looking forward to this at all. I looked at Martha with a concerned expression, got up and followed Sushi into the den where she curled up on a coach. I sat next to her and placed a hand on her. "Are you okay making this journey with us? And please don't lie to me. I can sense your anxiety."

Sushi raised her head. "Yes, I am anxious because even though I can shift into demon like creatures, the evil that comes along with it, the anger and need for violence is unappealing. It is not my true nature and I really don't want people to see that side of me, including myself."

"Well, since we already have a demon shifter in the midst, maybe you won't have to shift. I will need you and Sasha close to me to watch my back. I will be spending much of my concentration and energy trying to reach out to Lela. If something gets past the others, you can protect as you see fit. I will do what I can with what little magic I have. But you two are much stronger than I am."

"Thanks Aubrey. I appreciate that and will shift only if you are threatened." She let out a sigh and laid her head down again.

"Don't get too comfy. We are leaving shortly."

By the time I returned to the kitchen, it was clean. Martha was putting away the food leftover from breakfast. I leaned up against the counter. "I have some potions that could be of some help. I can get those packed up if we have time."

Martha said, "We can use all of the help we can get. Bring along anything that could be helpful. Also, please throw in some of your healing potions. I would like to for all of us to make it out alive."

On that note, I went back to my lab and started thinking about the best potions to bring along. One was to stop blood loss. The other for consciousness, and another to heal wounds. I also threw in a potion for invisibility which only offered a very temporary effect. Another was an acidic potion that I could use if something got too close to me for comfort. It could burn any demon enough to slow them down. Unless it was something very strong and then it may just piss them off.

Since I had transferred all my personal potions to small vials, I had enough room to pack several of each potion. I placed the vials in a leather belt according to its use and wrapped the belt around my waist. This would allow quick access to any potion I may need. Each vial had a different design on the lid which I had created and memorized so I would be able to identify each one quickly. Once I had completed my selections, I went to my room and gathered my backpack. By the time I reached the front foyer, both the girls and Martha were standing, ready to walk out the door.

I pulled the map out of my bag and said, "Let's take one last look at the map to make sure her last location remains the same."

"Good idea. But make it quick. The others are waiting."

Martha followed me to the dining room and I spread the map out again. I felt along the tunnel where we were to enter. Once my fingers reached the first pathway, my fingertips began to tingle. I closed my eyes and let me fingers follow the paths on the map. Suddenly, the sensation stopped and I opened my eyes. She had been moved a little deeper into the Underworld. My breath caught in my throat. "She has to be alive because her location has moved. This is a really good sign, right?" I looked at Martha for a response.

"It can mean that she is still alive. You should remain optimistic. It will help keep your mind open to her once we get close. You can try to communicate with her. You think she will recognize that it is you?"

"We had a nickname for each other. Maybe she will remember that." I folded up the map so only the area of the tunnel and Lela's potential location was easy to access. As I slipped it into my bag and threw the bag over my shoulder, Martha lifted both arms and the four of us were gone.

Next thing I knew, we were standing on a dirt path next to two large boulders. Across from us sat two young men and an older man who I recognized immediately to be Micca. I liked Micca when I had met him. He was down to earth, kind but quick to get to the point. He was very straight forward which I found refreshing. Outside of Martha, I had found that most people tended to beat around the bush. I hated that.

Martha introduced us. "Eric, Stan, this is Aubrey and her familiars Sushi and Sasha." As she spoke, Neme, Martha's familiar, appeared next to her and Martha leaned in on him. Eric was tall with short brown hair and had the greenest eyes I had ever seen. He was lean with muscle. Stan was a bit stockier and looked much older than the rest.

"Without time to get to know one another I expect only three things from the everyone except Aubrey. One, stay alive. Two, protect Aubrey. And three, rescue Lela, dead or alive." I quickly turned to Martha at the last remark. "Aubrey, I have to be realistic…. You, optimistic. Now let's head inside." Martha handed over her backpack to Stan and walked forward grabbing my arm in the process. My familiars walked on either side of me both in their normal form. Micca jumped up and joined Martha at her side and Eric and Stan took up the rear. At that point, Martha threw out her shield to include me and the girls.

The initial tunnel was steep and we walked downward until it finally opened into a huge cavern. Stalagmites, columns, and other formations covered the floors, walls and ceilings. The air was moist and made it difficult to breath. There was very little noise except those from our movements. As I entered the center of the room, a tingling sensation began to pull me to the right, down a wide pathway that moved deeper underground. I could hear a rumbling as we moved forward. Martha and Micca moved in front of me and Martha held out her arm to stop and be quiet. Behind me, I heard a sound like bones crunching together and water moving. I turned in time to watch Eric shift into something I had never seen of before. He was twice his original size and his skin was gray with almost a purplish hue. His entire body was covered in some sort of large thorns. He had formed two additional arms and both his legs and arms were taught with large muscles. His head matched the rest of his body. He was no longer Eric and it was nothing I would want to get into a fight with. I turned back to Martha, my eyes large. She just grinned and slowly began to move forward. I looked to each of my familiars and they both seemed unfazed.

I reached out with my mind and felt for Lela. All I could feel was anger, darkness and hint of sadness although the tingling continued. I think the other emotions were coming from those who had not chosen to be here. I blocked out the other emotions and put out the feeler for Lela. But I didn't feel Lela, only the tingling remained. I put my mental block back up. As I took my next foot forward, a demon stepped out in front of Martha and Micca. In sync, they both lifted their arms, mumbled something. The demon released a high-pitched squeal and then exploded. I lifted my arm to block my face from flying demon guts but Martha's shield held.

Martha whispered, "Well, that's not good. Now others will be aware of our presence. Everyone be on your toes. This could get ugly." Everyone nodded and we moved forward at a little faster pace.

As Martha and Micca cleared the path of curious demons, annihilating them one by one, the girls finally shifted into larger forms, Sasha and Sushi both shifting into identical Griffins. The smaller creatures that had moved into our path took one look at the girls and Eric and slithered back from where they came. It made Martha and Micca's job a little easier. Stan had his hands full for what appeared behind us, coming in from paths that led off to the left and right of us.

We continued to venture forward and then everything and everyone stopped. A cold breeze flushed the caverns and all the remaining creatures scattered off. The sound of something large began a high scream from further down below us.

As it got closer, I began to sense another human. I opened my mind. "Lela? Is that you? It's your little monkey."

"Brie?" I vaguely heard in my head. She remembered me. She was alive!

I started to walk forward and this time it was Micca that grabbed my arm and shoved me behind him. We heard a scrapping along the floor and the sound of chains rattling. I could feel Lela's pain through all the noise that was coming from within. Coming around the corner was the largest beast I had ever seen, which didn't mean much with my experience. It had a small head, a large midsection, and multiple limbs. The head was covered in blood and had something sticking out of its teeth which were large and pointed. It was hard to tell which were arms and which were legs as the creature was using three to walk, if you could consider it walking. It was the color of dark green and black splotches all over the skin. Several of the limbs contained pinchers like that of a crab. One of the arms had the end of a chain rapped around it and at the end of that chain lay what looked like Lela, being dragged along the ground. She looked up from the floor and into my eyes.

She mouthed, "Brie?".

I responded. "Oh Lela. Are you okay?"

I wanted to run to her but the beast had risen on two of its limbs and hovered over all of us as if we were just small pests that were in the way. It realized that Lela recognized me and became defensive, stepping backwards and placing a limb on top of Lela and hissed at us.

Out stepped Medea and she walked right into the arms of the creature as if it was her beloved pet. The creature threw a limb over her shoulder and caressed her chest. Medea groaned and said, "Not now dear. We have visitors to deal with." That interaction between those two made me shiver. It was a disgusting thought that the two could be intimate. Or maybe, it was just one sided. The creature focused all eyes on our little group. Even the size of the griffins or Eric's beast weren't enough to intimidate the creature.

Martha was the first to speak. "Ahh, Medea. I have heard much about you. We have come for the witch, Lela." She said as she pointed to where Lela laid.

Medea laughed. "And I of you Martha. You have slaughtered several of my friends. You will get nothing from me, especially the witch. You will have to go through me and my pet, Chinca."

"With friends like yours who needs enemies." Martha retorted. Not original but she said it, nonetheless. "So, I guess we're just going to have to take her away from you."

Medea laughed again. "Oh, I don't think so. She has come to be quite helpful to get me the things I want. I cannot give her up just like that."

Martha threw the first blow sending Medea flying. She landed on her feet laughing. "So, this is how you want to play it? Oh, this should be fun!"

Medea leaned back and, putting her whole body into it, threw two balls back at Martha and Micca. Martha's shields couldn't withstand the blast and they both went flying backwards to land on their butts.

Medea released a loud cackle. "So, you think you can out-power me and my pet? Hah!"

Martha got up and mumbled through gritted teeth, "Enough of this!" With everything she had, Martha sent a bolt of lightning at Medea striking both Medea and her pet simultaneously. Micca followed suit causing Medea and Chinca to stagger backwards.

Martha and Micca prepared themselves for the worse raising both their shields to protect the group.

In the meantime, I reached out to Lela and mentally asked her what I could do to help her. I asked her if she was strong enough to fight.

*"Brie, if you can just release these binds, I think I can get us out of here. I know Medea's weakness."* I relayed this to Martha and heard a click, releasing the lock on the chains holding Lela. Lela didn't move. Martha and Micca kept their eyes on Medea. Stan and Eric continued to fight off the beasts coming in from behind. Lela slowly started caressing the "foot" of the leg that rested upon her. Something was happening and I had no idea what was going on.

In the meantime, Martha and Micca exchanged glances and prepared to zap the crap out of Medea again. Just as they were powering up, something happened. Chinca grabbed hold of Medea around the neck and pulled her into him.

"What the hell?!?", she screamed. Lela had a hold of Chinca's leg and was sending signals up into its midsection which had turned to a beat red. Apparently, the animal was in heat, and Medea had been an easy mate. Medea tried to break free but the magic she used against the animal only intrigued it more. Its midsection began to throb and wrapped several legs around Medea pulling her even closer to his midsection.

Lela had freed a hand and sent a signal up into the nervous system of the animal initiating its constant physical need of Medea. Later, she told me how she watched the interaction of the two and realized that the animal was obsessed with Medea's power just as Medea had with Lela.

Martha jumped at the opportunity and went for Lela. She was fast. She dodged a leg and freed Lela from her chains. Lela was so skinny that it took nothing for Martha to pick her up, run back to us and waved her hand around in the air.

Medea screamed out. "You idiot. The witch is getting away. Leave me alone and get her back!"

Before Medea could say anymore, we were all standing outside the entrance in which we had come. We could still hear the screams coming from Medea. She was no match for her pet companion. Once I looked over Lela for any major injuries and had I determined she was relatively okay, Martha said that we had to scatter. As soon as Chinca had relieved himself, Medea would be hot on our heels.

Micca, Eric, Stan had zapped themselves out of there immediately. Martha got the rest of us back to my house. "Aubrey, you have to get you, the girls and your sister to a safe place quickly. Medea will come here first knowing where Lela had lived. Neme and I are headed back to the coast. The farther apart we are, could buy you more time. Good luck!" And she was gone.

## CHAPTER 8
### *THE ESCAPE*

"**A**H SHIT" WAS ALL I COULD SAY. I DIDN'T KNOW where we could go. I started thinking about what Max had last said to me. I tried to reach out to him with my senses and felt him instantly, which was unusual. That only seemed to work with family or someone close to me, like Martha. Next thing I knew, even before I could alert Lela, we were in a large stone room. It was furnished with a couch, armchairs and a couple of end tables with a front door to the right and a hallway that lead off to the left. I looked out the window next to the door and the moonlight reflected off the snow on the ground. It was cold outside, and I was not dressed for the weather. I dropped the backpack and removed my belt of potions. Lela saw me shiver and waved her arm. I was suddenly dressed in a heavy sweater over my t-shirt and jeans. Only after I was tended to did Lela do the same for herself. She had been wearing less than me until she changed into a long-sleeved tunic and some leggings and boots.

"Thanks." I hugged my sister and everything that just happened sent a flood of emotions. She hugged me back but didn't shed a tear. "Are you okay?" My voice broke as I tried to speak.

I was concerned for what had happened to her over all those years.

"I'm better now. Brie, why did it take so long for you to come for me?"

Guilt overcame me. "Lela, I am not as strong as you and I had to seek help from someone I could trust. That took time. Remember, I was only ten years old when you had been taken away and had no idea what happened to you. By the time I entered the University, I didn't even know if you were alive or how to find you." We had so much to talk about including everything that led to where we were currently located. "I have a lot to tell you."

Lela didn't respond to what I had just said. All she said was, "Where in the heck are we?" I got the impression she didn't want to press me further on the earlier subject until I was ready. I think she understood I did what and when I could.

"I have no idea but I'm pretty sure we are no longer in the United States." I said since it was late summer there and we were no place like that.

•　　•　　•

After finding something to eat and exploring our current domain, Lela grabbed a shower and we settled into the living area where a fire crackled in a fireplace and we talked. Surprisingly, Sushi curled up next to Lela. Lela and I talked for hours. Sasha laid close to the fireplace. Lela told me everything that had happened after she was taken away. It was awful. I was amazed at how resilient she seemed. You could see the last ten years in her eyes but that was the only sign of what she had been through. Her hair was longer and she was a lot taller than I remembered. Of course, so was I. She had that simple look with her straight blond hair, pale skin, and slim form. She looked better now that she had eaten.

I told her about the University, Martha, Max and how we ended up here. I was pretty sure that we were somewhere in the British Isle but not exactly where. I imagined I would see Max soon since I knew he was the one that brought us here. No sooner than I had that thought than there was a knock on the door. I immediately sensed it was Max. Maybe I was giving out feelers of my own and he could read my mind. I doubted it but I really didn't know just how much power he had even though I was pretty good at blocking things out.

I turned to Lela, "It's Max. Now you'll see what I have been telling you about. He is drop dead gorgeous! And there is something about him that I can't sense. I can't quite put my finger on it because he is more powerful than my empathic abilities but I sense there is more to him than he portrays." I got up and made my way to the door and looking back at Lela, she just smiled. I had never been attracted to anyone but she could see it on my face when I talked about him. I barely even knew this man.

I opened the door and my heart did a little flip. He looked so hot that it made me fumble for my words. "Uh, hey, come on in." I stood aside to let him in. I had never really dated but had a few male friends from school. I wasn't naïve, just inexperienced. How do you talk to someone when you feel yourself blushing at every word? I don't remember feeling this awkward when he came to the house.

With a wave of his arm, he dried his clothes and boots from the wet snow from outside. He nodded his head at me as a hello.

"I should have warned you about the weather but I didn't feel that you had a lot of time for explanations before I brought you here."

"That's okay. Lela took care of that for us plus there was already a fire blazing in the living room hearth. Please come and meet Lela." My eyes lingered on him before I moved. I think he caught my glare and gave a slight grin. His blue eyes and gentle facial features didn't match his broad shoulders and muscular physique. But, somehow, it worked on him.

Max followed me into the room where we had settled in. Sasha and Sushi raised their heads in acknowledgement and then laid their heads back down. "Max, this is my sister Lela. Lela, this is the sorcerer I have been telling you about."

Lela stood up and shook his hand. "I guess I have you to thank for getting us out of reach of Medea. I'm sure she is fuming by now."

"Not a problem. I knew you two would need a quick escape far from her feelers if you managed to get out. I was just waiting to hear from Aubrey."

Lela looked at me with a question in her eyes. I knew exactly what she was wondering. I turned to her. "I not only have excelled at blocking but I can also extend my own emotions and thoughts towards others if necessary. In addition to that, my witchcraft spells with potions have improved due to my training at the University. I had reached out for Max when we needed a place to hide." I explained.

She got that grin on her face whenever she was impressed. "You've become quite the Empath since I last saw you."

Max smiled. "Yes, and she is more talented than she realizes but that will come with more experience." He shed his coat and sat in one of the armchairs. A hot cup of coffee appeared on the table next to him. He picked it up and took a sip before he continued. "You have landed in one of my favorite little hideaways deep in the forests of the Southern Uplands of Scotland. I don't use it much anymore but had it ready for you just in case. I hope you have made yourself at home. You will stay here for a few days until you can get some rest but then we'll have to move on to the portal. I will explain everything in detail after you have had a good night's rest."

I thought about the home I just left and everything I ever knew. "What about the house? Any chance of going back there to pick up some things?"

Max shook his head. "Too risky. Make a list and I will have someone make sure those items aren't cursed and we can get them for you." I nodded my head. He continued. "I know I have said all of this before but it is pertinent that no one can find you. It was a big risk allowing you to bring your sister but I was willing to make that concession considering what I am asking of you."

Lela finally chimed in. "Can you tell me what this is all about?"

"I will fill you in on everything tomorrow. You two need to get some rest." Max started to rise.

"Will we be safe here, alone?" I would have rather he stayed but I wasn't going to push it. I had been alone for so long and I rather liked his company. There was something about him that thrilled me. I couldn't read him like most people so that was intriguing. Suddenly, I realized I had just been staring at him, saying nothing. My face flushed and he smiled. Finally, I got my tongue untied and wished him a good night.

After Max left, Lela made it quite clear that she could see how I felt. "I think he might have a slight crush on you too. Remember, he has been watching you a lot longer than you have known him."

"I have never felt like this about anyone. I mean he is very attractive."

"Attractive my ass. He is downright hot." Lela butted in.

"I know. I didn't give it much thought when we first met. It is odd how quickly I find myself this attracted to him. No one has had this kind of effect on me."

"No one?! Wow. At least there were some good-looking demons that I would come across and, as long as Medea was not using me for her evil games, I could have a little fun."

Unable to process her last comment, I just sighed. I got up. "Lela, I'm really tired and am going to find a comfy bed." I went to give her a hug and Sushi and Sasha followed me out of the room as I said goodnight. "It's good to have you back, Lela. Love you."

"Love you too sister. And thanks...for everything. It feels good to be free again."

•　　•　　•

Max showed up around ten the next morning. Lela and I were still having coffee and chatting in the living area. He was dressed in blue jeans that stuck into his low boots and a blue sweater which brought out the blue in his eyes. His jeans were tight showing a fine outline of his ass. Once again, I found myself having difficulty taking my eyes off him. His eyes seemed to twinkle when he looked at me. I poured him a cup of coffee as he settled into one of the armchairs. Lela and I sat at opposite ends of the couch with Sasha and Sushi curled up between us.

Max cleared his throat. "It's time I get you up to date on where things stand so far and why we are in much need of an Empath and another Healer." He spoke of the prophecy and the Soluzari. He explained about their power but their limited ability to communicate with us. That was where I came in. I thought I was pretty good at translating peoples' feelings into words but Max indicated that it was more of a telepathic ability. He also explained that in case of injuries, they would need someone who could learn and help to heal these other worldly creatures. I would be working with a Shifter Healer to help guide me through the process to understand and help these creatures.

"Oh, before I forget, the items you requested should arrive at your new home later today." I had wanted the book of potions that my grandmother had given to me, some of my more difficult healing potions that I had already produced. Max continued. "Also, your new home will be well equipped including new wardrobes, food supplies and other amenities that you may need. Anything else can be purchased at the local shops not far from where you both will live. Do you have any questions for me?"

I wanted to know more about this new species he referred to as the Soluzari. "Can you tell me more about these people you speak of?"

"Well, we don't know much as we have had a little difficulty communicating. They are a gentle race, small in size and very different from you and me. Their speech is limited but we have managed to gather some of their history. There are a little over a hundred of them that have arrived here in their escape from a planet that, what we think, was destroyed in some sort of a meteor shower. Very few escaped but those that did had set course for our galaxy and our planet. They landed not far from the house of the Overseers. This had all been indicated in an old prophecy and even though we weren't sure of the timing, we were prepared for their arrival, fortunately."

I thought of how exciting this must be for the Overseers and my curiosity was peeked. I just didn't feel I was the one to help these people. I was just fresh out of the University and still coming into my own. I still didn't know the extent of my powers.

Lela had a few questions of her own and after Max had answered most of them, we decided to take a break and get some lunch. By the time I made it to the kitchen, the table had already been set and food sat out to be served. I wasn't sure which of them was responsible but I was pretty sure it was Lela. Since Max had no plans to leave anytime soon, he joined us. I was glad he was sticking around for the day, although, I kept my guard up with my emotions. I did not want to give off any sign about my attraction for him. It would be easy to let my guard down around him. He was easy to be around. I did catch him once watching me out of the corner of my eye during lunch. It sent chills down my spine.

Lela spent the days recovering from her time in the Underworld. We spent most of our time communicating through telepathy as I needed the practice. I did not know what to expect with the Soluzari. Max was in and out but spending much time with me, trying to prepare me for what was in store. He explained about the other people that inhabited the island, witches, warlocks, and shifters. He let me know that all the people there were there entirely to support the health and welfare of the Soluzari and of course, each other. The witches and warlocks were in place as protectors of the portal and the new species and provided for the entire population. The shifters were the backbone of the infrastructure. I would be introduced to the Soluzari after a week or two after following the local Healer and get a feel for her process when tending to the locals. Max indicated that my background in potions would come in handy for the entire population and just another reason that I am well-suited for the position.

Lela recovered quickly and her powers regenerated themselves after much needed food and rest. Sushi and Sasha seemed to go with the flow of the whole thing as if this was their destiny all along. I was told by Max that they had been sent to protect and look after me and they would continue to support me as necessary.

The day of the move through the portal, I was a bit apprehensive but felt better prepared for what was to come. We all gathered in the front room once the sun set and Max transported us to the base of the portal which was surrounded by two stones that sat about ten feet high and apart by five feet. There was no indication that anything existed on the other side of those stones except a hill that led upwards but once we stepped though the two stones, we were immediately swept away.

# CHAPTER 9
## *FATIMIA*

I LOST MY FOOTING IN THE SAND AND LANDED ON MY BUTT on the other side. The girls landed on their feet, of course, and chuckled at my typical clumsiness. It was early daylight on the island. The water was a gorgeous aqua color and as clear as day. I had never seen anything like it. Where the beach ended, the woods began. There was a small dirt road that led into the woods. A minivan sat at the edge of the woods.

Max smiled. "Welcome to the island of Fatimia ladies. I will take you to your new home and then we can meet for lunch in town. It would be good that you meet some of the locals as soon as possible. Everyone is expecting to meet all of you today but we will have to see how that goes. I'll drop you off at your house first, as I have some business to attend to. I would also like to take you out on a tour so you can see all that the island has to offer. Then, Aubrey, we will go to meet the Healer. She is expecting you." Max turned to the portal and spoke some kind of spell.

Everyone gave me a chance to stand up and brush myself off before following Max to the van. Lela and the girls jumped into the back while I climbed into the passenger seat up front. I kept quiet, taking it all in. It was surreal considering the quiet and lonely life I had led in the past. I had been so sheltered from the realities of the world. Things were moving fast.

Max headed away from the beach and, what I could gather from the location of the sun, headed west. We passed several neighborhoods, according to Max, owned by the shifter population. After driving about 30 miles inland, the view converted from suburbia to downtown. First, a restaurant or two and then more and more shops of various goods. There was none of the big-name stores that you saw in the bigger towns and cities in the U.S. There was no multipurpose shopping. All the businesses were individually owned and run and all had their own specialty, Max indicated.

We slowed down as we traveled through downtown Fatimia. Max waved at a few passer-byes. We finally turned off the main road through town and took a couple of turns and traveled to a more wooded area. "We are now located on the northeastern side of the island and you are not far from the beach north of your property. It isn't a large island but enough for this sorcerer." Max explained as he finally pulled in front of a familiar home. Our home! Max had moved our entire house from Arkansas to Fatimia. Something inside me relaxed. "Oh Max, this is the best I could ever have hoped for!"

Max smiled. "I thought you could use a little touch of home after the last couple of weeks."

"I don't know how you managed this but this is awesome! Even has wooded surroundings like home."

"Well, the island is your home now and I wanted to make it feel that way. I hope this was acceptable." Max said as he came to a stop right in front of our childhood home.

I turned to Lela and she seemed pleased. I was glad she was comfortable coming back to the very place she was sent away from. Sasha managed to squeeze out the front passenger door as soon as I opened it. She ran up the front steps yowling in appreciation and the front door opened in time for her to leap inside without breaking her stride. Sushi walked behind with the rest of us. Max walked us to the door to make sure everything was kosher and then bowed out to go take care of his business.

I turned to watch him walk away. As soon as he reached the bottom of the front steps, he was gone. I paused and then turned to Lela and said, "Yay!", gave her a hug, and headed back to my lab. Everything was still in place just as I had left it. "Oh, by the way, I turned Mom and Dad's room into a laboratory." I yelled at Lela from down the hallway.

"That works for me more than you know." Lela laughed. She was in the process of using her magic to redecorate her bedroom since I had given her access to one of the banking accounts to do with what she wanted. Afterall, Nana had left it for the two of us and I had my earnings from over the years stashed away in another account.

I watched how easy it was for her and asked her to do the same for my room. I could use an upgrade myself. Lela would disappear and then reappear with new furniture. "You make magic look so easy. What little I can do is usually connected to one of my potions." She also turned the extra bedroom into a lounging room for the girls with beds that sat just inside of the base of the windows where they could sun themselves. They loved the heat. "Can you upgrade the den as well? I would have refurnished before if I had had the where with all." She went through a couple of designs of couches and chairs until she finally decided on a nice white leather set.

The kitchen was well supplied so we didn't have to worry about that anytime soon. We left the dining room and living room alone since we rarely spent any time in those rooms. Everything was coming together quite nicely. Everyone grabbed a small snack and laid down for a quick nap.

I woke up about 11am and jumped in the shower. It was much warmer on the island during the day so I put on cooler clothes for our lunch and the tour with Max. Max had wanted all of us to go along so the locals would have a chance to meet the whole lot of us. By the time I had showered and dressed, Max had arrived. I had put on some casual shorts and a loose white button-down blouse and some sneakers. I was not sure what we were in store for so I thought casual was the best option. Fatimia seemed like that kind of place.

Max had also change into long shorts, a button-down shirt and boat shoes. With his dress code down a few notches, I felt much more comfortable around him. "Hi." was all I could manage when I saw him sitting in our newly refurbished den. He had a nice tan and, with his boyish features, looked perfectly normal but I knew he carried a lot of power.

"How did you get all this new furniture in so quickly?" Max asked as he looked around with a concerned look on his face.

"Lela redecorated some of the rooms, removing old familiar furniture. I think she needed an upgrade."

"That's fine but where did it come from?" Max voice got a little deeper, more concerned. "We cannot bring anything onto the island without it fully vetted by our group of witches and warlocks."

Lela came into the room in good spirits. "Oh, no worries, Max. I noticed a furniture store on the way in and made some exchanges. I briefly spoke to the store owner and paid him generously for allowing me to switch out the old with new stuff."

"That works perfectly. Thanks for keeping your magic local. I cannot emphasize that enough now that we are here. Also, to both of you, no contacting anyone on the other side of the portal. It's too risky and you both will be busy enough for a while." Max seemed to have something on his mind so no one said anything. He continued. "Lela, I have a proposition for you. Would you be interested in training our younger witches about the Underworld and how to recognize threats? Your previous experience could come in quite handy in keeping the island protected from anyone entering the portal that may have demonic tendencies. We like to keep travel to the fourth dimension at a minimal until we can become fully self-sufficient."

Lela was more than happy to have some responsibility. "It would be a pleasure to tutor the younger witches about the Underworld. It is important that they are able to recognize evil magic quickly."

"Thanks, Lela. I thought you would be a perfect fit for something like this at the local school. You'll have time to prepare your course work before school opens in a couple of weeks. I will have one of the local witches contact you to get you acquainted with our training programs here on the island." Max then turned to me. "You and I need to talk before I introduce you to the Soluzari. Please keep tomorrow morning open for some one-on-one time."

Max looked at his watch. "I guess we better get going if we are to beat the lunch crowd." Since everyone was ready to go, we all got up and headed out the front door. Max and I were the last to go out the front door and he placed his hand on my lower back to guide me out, shutting the door behind him. Chills rushed up my spine at his touch. I thought I hid it well but he smiled so I knew I had been caught. I let down my walls to get a sense of what he was feeling. I flushed at what I had felt. Then I heard a voice inside my head, *"Careful, my little Empath."* No one else heard a thing. I immediately put my walls up to block out any further telepathic communication.

This telepathy thing was becoming a habit with me and I didn't understand why. Being an Empath always allowed me to sense how others felt but to actually hear their thoughts was an entirely different ballgame. I always thought the connection I shared with my sister was unique. But then there was Martha. That had been unusual but I hadn't given it much thought. Maybe that's why Max wanted me here. He said that there was a communication gap with the Soluzari.

We turned into the restaurant shortly before noon. The crowd was getting thick but we went right in and got a table immediately. Everyone turned and watched us make our way to our table. Sasha and Sushi pounced over to the table and sat down before any of us. They didn't even wait to be seated. Lela, Max and I followed suit. I looked out at the crowd and found all eyes on us.

A large woman walked over to our table. "Good afternoon, Max. So, who are your guests today?" I was sure she already knew who we were. I was pretty sure she was just being polite but I didn't let down my walls to find out. I was locked up tighter than a drum.

"Hi Judy. This is Aubrey, her sister Lela and Aubrey's familiars, Sasha and Sushi. I believed I mentioned that Aubrey would be arriving today."

"That's right. I forgot all about it. Welcome to our little corner of paradise. My name is Judy Le Pew and am, along with my husband, the proprietor."

"Thank you and pleased to meet you," Lela replied. I just smiled feeling a little skittish at all the eyes on me. I knew I was here for something important but I was not used to any attention.

We had a chance to meet many of the shifters that worked downtown. Especially a broad-shouldered shifter named Michael who seemed to take a liking to Lela. Finally, after lunch and many introductions, we headed out to tour the island. The island measured fifty miles north to south and seventy miles in length. It was surrounded by beautiful blue water with smaller outlying islands off to the south where no one lived. The western side of the island was mostly rainforest which ran up the large mountain-side to a single peak on the island. Max drove up halfway where we got out and had a chance to see most of the island. It was beautiful to see the lush island and its surrounding waters.

Max pointed upward, "I reside at the top and have a view of the entire island. Along the base of the mountain below, most of the witches and warlocks each have laid claim to a portion of land that surrounds the entire mountain to protect the Soluzari who have taken up residence on the west side of the mountain about halfway up."

"Are we going to visit the Soluzari today?" I asked.

"No, not today. It will take a while and you need the whole day to spend with them."

Our tour took us around the base of the mountain where most of the witches and warlocks resided. Max explained that there was some intermingling of the shifters and the witches but the warlocks mostly kept to themselves and to their duties since the inception of the island which only occurred a couple of years earlier. The entire population was relatively new and built up quickly in preparation of the Soluzari.

By the time we returned to the house, it was late in the afternoon. Max wanted to at least introduce me to the local Healer so I could begin my studies with her immediately. He dropped off Lela and the girls since it would take a couple of hours. The car ride to the Healer's residence/business was not far and we rode in silence, mostly due to the little embarrassment that occurred leaving the house earlier that day.

After traveling the north road along the coast and thirty minutes later, we arrived at the home of Rigada, the Healer. She was an older witch with thick brown curly hair. She was rather thin but a prominent woman in her own right. She intimidated me a little when she said "*Hello*" without saying a word. I immediately went double time on my blocking when she finally spoke. "Strong Empath for such a young lady."

I noticed that she emphasized the word Empath when she said it. It was as if she was inferring something else and I didn't want to believe what I thought it might be. I let it go. "Hello, it's a pleasure meeting you" was all I could manage. Although this woman was thin, she was very tall and I was petite compared to her height, although, I was petite to most everyone I had encountered. We sat and discussed my studies. We planned to meet every day over the next week so I would have more knowledge using my potions for healing purposes. After several hours of reviewing what I did know about healing potions, Rigada excused herself to tend to other business. Max and I headed back to my house in silence once again.

I was taking in all that was happening: having my sister back, the move, the new training. I guess it was better than being stuck in the rut I had fallen in to in Lonesboro. My thoughts were quickly broken when Max piped up."

"I guess you are wondering about your ability to read my thoughts when your guard is down?"

"I have my theory but don't understand why it is happening so often now."

"Then I will confirm it. You are telepathic and have been since birth. You were trained at an early age to block out any outside feedback as an Empath. But that also blocked your telepathic tendencies. As you have noticed, only when you let your guard down are you able to hear others. And usually, those others are much stronger witches than you are able to block. Now that you are surrounded by magic, your abilities will be pressed and even more so when you meet the Soluzari. They are a telepathic species and you will be the main communicator with them."

I mumbled, "I figured as much." I knew there was more to this at the beginning but hadn't pieced it together. "It had become more frequent with more powerful beings. For instance, the Healer was immediately able to communicate with me even with my shields up. Why is that?"

"You are a strong Empath but will need to use more energy to block out those that are also prevalent in telepathy unless you choose otherwise." Max replied. "This is the main reason I brought you into the fold. In addition with your training as a healer, you will provide a great service to the Soluzari." We pulled into the driveway of the house.

"If Rigada is a healer and telepathic, why not just use her to communicate with the Soluzari?"

"Good question. Our shifter community takes up most of her time. She has very little to spare for the Soluzari and they will require a designated person for not just physical healing but also with any other issues they may have with our world. That's where your empathic abilities will come in handy. You will be able to detect any discontent among them and help them understand our ways better. You can show them what pain and other earthly emotions feel like. It will help them understand us better. Does that make any sense?"

"I guess."

"If you have any issues with any of this, please let me know now. Your grandmother had approved of my approach with you and I hope that you are on board one hundred percent."

"I have to admit, everything is happening so quickly but I'm up for the challenge." I sat up straight and took a deep breath. "Max, thank you for trusting me with all of this. When will I get to meet the Soluzari?"

Max smiled. He was pleased with my response. "Soon enough Aubrey. Now, I must get back to my duties but will be in touch in a couple of days. Take some time to meet more of the townspeople and discover the island. Go relax on the beach. You will be busy soon enough."

Max and I got out of the car and walked toward the house. I turned back to Max as I reached the front door, "Thanks again,

Max….for everything. Have a good evening." I smiled not waiting for him to respond and went inside. I didn't want to linger any more than necessary. I had a full plate and falling for this sorcerer would not be a good idea. Max watched as I shut the front door behind me before he disappeared.

C HAPTER 10

## *THE MEETING*

ELA, SUSHI, SASHA AND I HAD A COUPLE OF DAYS TO settle in and get to town for a walkabout. We met many of the shifters that ran the shops we stopped into. The island on a whole contained a small population similar to that of a small township. The shifter population lived in close proximity of one another and lived on the east side of the island. We had neighbors but it was a little hike. It was a married couple between a witch and a shifter and a rare unity at that. It wasn't that the different species didn't get along they just had different focuses. The shifter community was mainly focused on the infrastructure of Fatimia and tended to be more sociable.

Lela worked on her curriculum for the younger witches, the ones that came over with their parents before the Shift. She had also met a shifter named Michael who she began to see as often as her time permitted.

We had a little mishap when Sasha and Sushi got a little bit bored and began playing jokes on one another. Then, Sasha shifted into a chipmunk and triggered Sushi's attack reflex. All was well until Sasha couldn't shift back. Then I heard squeaking and yowling coming from outside. I found that Sushi had chased Sasha under the porch and got her head stuck in the hole also blocking Sasha from her only exit. Lela managed to get Sushi's head free but we couldn't figure out how to help Sasha return to normal. By the time we contacted Max for help, Sushi had gotten a hold of Sasha, the chipmunk, and began tossing her around like a toy. Sasha finally smartened up and played dead until Sushi lost interest. Once Max was able to figure out what went wrong with Sasha's shifting powers, due to the abnormal atmosphere of this dimension, Sasha was able to shift back to her feline form. To say the least, Sasha was pretty pissed with Sushi even though she brought it on herself. It was days before those two spoke again.

I began following Rigada on her cases, and a shifter with a shattered leg was the first. Typically, they could shift and heal small fractures on their own. Unfortunately for the shifter, this particular break was too damaged to heal correctly without some help. I watched Rigada reset it, moving all the small bone fragments into their proper place. She used her magic to find each piece of bone, medicinal potions for pain, and magic to bind the bones back together. The guy was up and walking within a couple of hours albeit a small limp. I was amazed at how easy it was for Rigada. In addition to watching her work, we only spoke telepathically. She insisted that I learn to block out the feelings but still communicate. When she was resetting the bone, I accidently forgot to put up my shields up and felt the pain of the shifter. He handled it better than I did.

•    •    •

After several days of working with Rigada, I was resting in the den when Max stopped in for a visit and to discuss the meeting with the Soluzari. "Why can't Rigada care for the Soluzari? She seems to have all of the attributes you need to communicate." I wasn't sure I was the right fit for the job.

"There is so little we know of these creatures and we need someone who can spend a hundred percent of their time with them. Rigada is not an Empath and limited in her telepathic abilities. She does not have the control and the intensity that you possess. As I have told you before, you are the strongest Empath I know and you will be able to sense things that the Soluzari may not be able to put into words." Max responded.

"Oh" was all I could say. I never thought about it that way but it made sense. "So, can you tell me more about them? What to expect?"

"I can tell you all I know." Max described the species, their features, their temperament and what little history he knew. "We are counting on you to clarify the details of what we do and don't know."

"Are they willing to communicate with a complete stranger?" I wasn't so sure of my abilities but my frequent telepathic conversations with my sister had given me more confidence.

"Your nature will eliminate any trepidations that they may have. You are very personable.

"Thanks."

"You also can explain to them the evil that lurks among our kind and I can demonstrate to them how to detect evil intentions." Max seemed confident that I could do this and, even though I knew very little about him, I trusted him implicitly. This was an odd feeling because I typically trusted no one.

"Are you ready to go meet them next week? I would like to at least make introductions."

"That works for me. I am as ready as I will ever be. Also, I am finding that I seem to have more time on my hands now that I quit making and selling my potions." I was anxious to meet these creatures. I had seen shifters of all kinds, demons, a troll and a few other of the paranormal species but never an alien species that was new to our planet. Max's description of the Soluzari made me very curious and a little excited.

• • •

The following week, we drove to the west base of the mountain and Max stopped the car. We got out and made our way to a wooded area where several paths moved off in varying directions. We took the one to the left. I walked beside Max until the trail got steeper and then I fell slightly behind.

"So why are we walking up and not using magic?" I finally asked.

"I don't want to surprise them until they are comfortable with us."

I couldn't really complain. The view was spectacular. Max had on snug blue jeans and light weight shirt that billowed in the breeze. As we hiked higher, making our entrance audible, the growth thickened with tropical trees and plants. We reached an opening and the forests gave way to a small open pasture. Floating from one place to another were busy little Soluzari, building their own little city within the woods. They moved delicately in everything they did. It would be easy to underestimate their power. Once they came into eyesight of

Max, the ones that were not in the middle of a project came running (more like floating) over. They gathered around Max making small sounds. Apparently, Max had built up quite a rapport with them.

I could sense a variety of emotions but mostly excitement in meeting someone new. Underneath that excitement laid a thin film of distrust. I hoped that I could change that for them by letting them know that we were on their side, to accept and protect the Soluzari that were so different than anything else that existed on earth.

Max took a step back and announced my presence. "Dear Soluzari, I would like for you to meet a very special person, Aubrey McHale. I spoke of her on my last visit."

One of the Soluzari approached me and tried to speak. It was a high-pitched squeak of a hello. I decided to let my walls down and a swarm of voices entered my head. "*Whoa, slow down. I am new at this so please, one at a time.*"

Once they realized that I was telepathic, one of the Soluzari who approached me smiled. "*I am so pleased to make your acquaintance. My name is Sahara, the queen of my people. Max has told us so much about you.*" Even though not a verbal word was said, I understood everything she was saying. Between what they had learned from reading our materials at the Overseers, it didn't surprise me that they already had a grip on our vocal language even though their pronunciation was thick with an unusual high-pitched accent.

Something about my abilities allowed me to translate what they could not form into words. I had been able to do that in other languages but I thought it was just my exposure to different languages of the old potion spells of my grandmother's. The older spells were often in other languages and she would read them to me and I would translate them myself. She had had the same ability which made her so effective in her work around the world.

*"Hello Sahara. The pleasure is all mine. Are you finding everything you need?"* Sahara's eyes were a grayish-blue and twinkled when she talked. She had pale blue, translucent skin to match. You could see down to the muscles that formed her body. Between her ears, she had a thick pile of long silver hair that fell down her back. She was actually beautiful even with her cat like features.

Max had made a point of listing things he wanted me to cover when communicating with the Soluzari. People as powerful as the Soluzari should be able see the aura of evil around that being but there were no guarantees that they could. Max had told me about that but I had my own empathic abilities to detect evil which I didn't sense in the Soluzari. I learned to sense evil when Medea had first appeared in our home.

I explained my purpose there and asked if there was a healer among them. Sahara replied, *"We have little use for a healer as you call it but we do have someone who specializes in physical medicine. In our world, there were not illnesses or diseases like you have here, or so I have read."*

Another Soluzari stepped forward and introduced herself. In a high-pitched voice, she attempted to speak. "I specialize in medicine for our people. My name is Hajara. I would be glad to work with you to teach you about our physical make-up." Hajara had the same translucent skin as Sahara but had a tinge of aqua color with eyes to match. Her long blond hair flowed much like Sahara's and most other females.

"Thank you, Hajara. I believe that you and I will be spending a lot of time together. I have a lot to learn from you."

I had forgotten that they had access to most all information of our world that is contained within the walls of the Overseers. I had learned through Max that they likely knew more than I did about our world, including all the facts about the other species within our planet. What they didn't know was the nature of some of those species in terms of greed and lies.

Sahara continued, *"Since the propensity for violence in your world is unheard of in ours, I understand that we have to remain under your protection until we can acclimate among your kind."*

*"This is very true."* I responded. I told her, and the others that had settled around us, the story of my sister and how she been bought and abused, all for greed, both by my parents and by Medea. Once I had finished my story of the sale and recovery of Lela, the nervous chatter had settled into a silence and the only noise was the business of the others as they were building their homes. I sensed shock among them as they couldn't really understand why one would want or need to do this to another.

Eventually, I was introduced to each one of the Soluzari and we began the journey of learning to communicate in my native language. After an afternoon of fielding questions and teaching certain phrases in English, practicing on their pronunciation, I was mentally exhausted. I was glad when Max returned us to the car with a swift wave of his hand and not have to hike the trail back down the mountain. We returned to my house in silence, although I still had some nervous energy left.

CHAPTER 11
## *THE THREAT*

JUST AS I ARRIVED AT THE HOUSE, I HEARD LELA IN MY head, before we entered, "*We may have a problem. Medea has somehow found the cabin where we first escaped in the hills of Scotland. She has hired some help from some pretty shady characters and is hot on my heals.*"

I relayed the message to Max not wanting to keep anything from him. We quickly entered the house to find Lela and a couple of shifters, Mikah and Keith, a warlock, Hadjie, and another local witch named Jona sitting around the dining room table with my map from Martha spread out in front of them. Apparently, once Jona, the first witch of the defense of the island, got word that Medea had found the cabin, she immediately came to find Lela to ask her how Medea could possibly track her that far. Jona was dressed in red conservative shorts outfit and had long, straight black hair. Mikah and Keith were two of the faster and more experienced lion shifters and both headed up the shifter defense of the island. Mikah was tall with shoulder length hair of a golden blond. He wore khaki shorts and a t-shirt tucked in. His broad shoulders and muscled arms and legs just showed how strong he could be. Keith carried a similar build but had longer, darker blond hair that was pulled back in a ponytail. He was dressed in a dress shirt with khaki shorts, a little cleaner cut than Mikah.

Lela had to explain to Jona that, after several attempts to escape, Medea had created a spell to track Lela but Lela had been able to break the spell, or so she thought. With all that was going on, Lela had forgotten to inform me or Max of this fact, thinking it not an issue. After a quick detection spell by Jona, we had come to find out that the tracking spell had been placed on me during the confrontation in the Underworld which wore off when we went through the portal but left a residue that allowed Jona to detect it. So that is why Medea had not used more power to fight for Lela. Medea knew that where I was, Lela was sure to be.

Max and I quickly joined the others around the map. Max swept his hand flat across the air in front of him and the picture that appeared showed Medea and two others working on a spell around the cabin, obviously trying to get possible remnants of where we could have headed from there. Since Max had transported Lela and I to the portal and his magic left no residue, the trail appeared to die there.

We knew Medea would not stop and the portal could be in jeopardy. Immediately, Max summoned the witches and warlocks of the island to our house. Someone so determined and powerful as Medea, the portal could be at risk and the exposure of the Soluzari would be eminent. I knew I had to give the Soluzari a crash course in evil and Lela could help by letting everyone know Medea's weaknesses. After spending years with the dark woman, Lela had watched Medea and learned as much as she could about her.

I was told to return to the Soluzari and let them know of the threat. I grabbed a small flask of green liquid meant to expose whatever truth I was trying to explain. I wasn't too worried about the idea I had to sick Sushi on them out of the blue to just to see how quick they were to react. I learned about the potion from my Nana to expose any threat that had triggered my senses but not shown themselves. The three of us (Sasha, Sushi, and I) each had our own methods for dealing with the paranormal which was initially identified by me long before they appeared. Very seldom would Sushi have to shift to her demon form in order to battle evil and seemed to be able to take care of herself regardless. All of us together could more than take care of ourselves in an attack.

Sushi, Sasha, and I jumped in the car and headed out. Whatever power the Soluzari had would be of little use if caught by surprise, or so I thought. We made record time back to the mountain and into Soluzari territory. Sushi stayed behind in the woods and Sasha stayed with her until I could formally introduce them. I reached the opening where the Soluzari had settled. Sushi was in the woods shifting into her beast form.

Sahara immediately approached me sensing my urgency. "A potential threat has been identified in our dimension and we have to be prepared if the portal is breached." I said quickly.

"What kind of threat?" Sahara replied as the others begin to gather around us. She was communicating with them telepathically but I could not detect what she was saying. I was locked up tighter than a bank vault and was not ready to open up until I was sure I could handle a bunch of babbling creatures.

"One of the worse kinds. I will tell you all I know but my sister can explain in more detail when she arrives. Lela, my sister, is giving the locals as much information she can so they can prepare at the portal on both sides."

I began telling them the short version of Medea and her tracking of us back to the British Isles. I also used the green liquid to give them a visual of Medea. "If Medea finds out you exist and the power you contain, we could have an entire lot of evil upon us in no time. The Underworld would imprison you and use you for who knows what and that would be very bad." As soon as I finished, Sahara was verbally barking out orders and people were scurrying about.

"Do you have any ability to protect yourself from unseen forces?" I asked quickly. Next thing I knew, I was staring at an open field, empty of the Soluzari even though I could still sense them. This was what I had anticipated before I left the house.

I opened my mind and felt for Sahara. *"Sahara? Are you there?"* I wasn't sure if they had relocated or put some kind of shield up or each Soluzari became invisible.

*"I am still in front of you, Aubrey."*

Sushi suddenly burst out into the opening in her beast form and Sasha followed. Immediately the beast and Sasha were blasted off their feet and back into the woods. I realized then that the Soluzari could protect themselves in a surprise attack.

*"Don't be alarmed! The beast and the feline are with me!"* I quickly yelled.

*"Are they a threat? Our shields do not seem to faze them."*

"They are my familiars, my protectors, and my friends, Sushi and Sasha." Sasha and Sushi, in her feline form, returned to my side.

All of the Soluzari were invisible to me, but, apparently, not to the girls. Sasha immediately started sniffing around, moving out the way as if someone was there. Strangely, Sushi moved towards the area where I last saw Sahara standing and laid down before her. Many of the Soluzari started making a squeaking sound around the girls and to my surprise, the girls responded in kind. Then the Soluzari reappeared. That's when I realized that the girls had a lot of physical similarities that the Soluzari had. The shape of their faces was very much alike and their ears were identical. I wondered if the girls could possibly be a far relative of the Soluzari.

"What is going on Sushi, Sasha?"

"These are our long-lost ancestors. We thought they had died out. Our genetics have mutated to become the felines we are today. We have gradually adapted to the human race and became very good at getting food, protection, and care." Sasha said with a wink. "At first, we bonded with witches and warlocks and could blend in well but then as poor genetics stepped in, we begin to lose our powers and our memories. Only those of us who have maintained a relationship with the paranormal world have kept most of our powers. We never thought we would see our heritage so intact."

"I felt Sahara's power as queen and knew she was **our** queen." Sushi lifted her head upward towards Sahara, her eyes gleaming with tears.

I didn't know what to say so I let the girls take in the Soluzari as their own and fell back in thought. I knew there was something special about Sushi and Sasha but I had not been able to put my finger on it. I never really knew their power base but I had some suspicion. For that matter, the entire domestic feline community always made me suspicious. How easy it was that they found a home and someone to care for them. Often, I would find Sasha up on her hind legs and I thought she was just being silly. Unbeknownst to me, that was her true nature. I found it amazing how we mutated and adapted to our surroundings over time.

I turned my attention to the group to the right of me. Sushi was deep in a conversation of sorts with a woman who carried a cane. With my brow raised at Sasha, I inquired, "Who is that?"

"That is their historian, Dinata. Sushi is telling her some facts about the feline species here on earth. I imagine she will have her hands full this point forward."

I looked up at the crowd that had gathered around us. "I think it best that we return back to the house to get the latest update on Medea."

A large female stepped forward. She had auburn hair with an orange tinge to her translucent skin. "I would like to join you along with Frech and Tomas," she pointed to two other males who had joined her at her side. "My name is Adinosa. We are the head of defense remaining of our kind. We may have something to offer in terms of strategic planning."

I looked at Frech and Tomas. They looked alike with their short blond hair spiked between their ears. Much like Adinosa, they had a larger muscular structure beneath the skin, "I will bring you along but cannot promise anything. Max seems to want to keep you well hidden." I paused, thinking that it couldn't hurt to bring them along. It would be a good indication of their defensive techniques.

Tomas and Sushi got caught up in a discussion on the way to our house about the deterioration of the feline species on earth and how they had come to be domesticated. My theory was that they had watched other species interact with humans and that is how they came to be domesticated. Pretty smart if you ask me. I still wonder if their great secret is that they do understand humans but chose not to make contact.

"We go back thousands of years so it does not surprise me that our kind had populated your planet at some point." Adinosa explained. "The domesticated descended from what your people call *Felis Silvestris* and they were descended from us."

"I wonder why you weren't able to retain your original features and powers?" Sushi asked.

"Thousands of years will do that to a species. Think about how far the humans have come from the neanderthal. It took them thousands of years to evolve to what they have become today. It is possible that the paranormal species on earth have mutated to become the different species that exist here."

"I know that our current form has existed here for thousands of years but did not think that our ancestors, would be so different than us." Sushi looked up at Adinosa as she floated above the seat. "Do you ever walk on the surface or do you always levitate above the ground?"

"We naturally float. It takes effort to stand on the surface. Your gravity does not seem to have any effect on us. Standing on the surface inhibits us from moving quickly when necessary." As the conversation died down, we arrived at our house.

CHAPTER 12

## THE PLAN

W E PULLED UP INTO THE DRIVE AND I NOTICED THAT
there were a few more cars than before. It appeared that
our house had become the headquarters for the attack on Medea.
I wasn't sure if it was acceptable that I brought the Soluzari along
but they had refused to discuss it.

When we entered through the front door, there was a room
full of witches, warlocks, and the two shifters I had met earlier.
Keith and Mikah were discussing something with Max. Max was
shaking his head. His eyes met mine and he winked. My stomach did a little flip and then it occurred to me that he didn't
seem too concerned about the current threat or the fact that I
had brought the Soluzari to the meeting. His emotions were
calm but serious. At this point, it was only a threat for Lela, not
the Soluzari.

A wide range of formidable characters were in our living room
and dining room, talking and laughing as if nothing was going
on. The island attitude seemed to have that effect on everyone I
had met so far. Everyone, except for Jona in her fancy outfit, was
dressed as casual as their attitudes and all eyes were on us.

I turned to the rest of the room and cleared my throat. "Excuse me. I would like to introduce the head of the Soluzari's defense." I turned to Adinosa. "This is Adinosa and their strategists, Tomas and Frech." I turned back to the group. "I know a few of you already."

The man closest to me stood up. "I am Stephan and this is Johan, also a warlock like myself." Stephan pointed to the man who immediately stood up next to him. They nodded their heads at the Soluzari and sat back down.

Another man stood with his hand up, "Hadjie." and returned to his seat without another glance towards the Soluzari that stood beside me. I sensed some hostility from him and wondered what was it that got under his skin. I would wait until I had a moment alone with Max to ask him about it.

The last stranger in the room was another witch that was still caught up in an argument with Jona about destroying Medea on the spot. Jona held her hand up to stop the woman in midsentence and turned to me and my crew.

"Hi Aubrey." She turned her gaze to the three Soluzari. "I am Jona and this is my sister, Briatta. I am surprised to see you here."

Adinosa stepped forward before I could explain, "We thought it best if we brought our expertise to the table and felt that you should not fight our battles on your own."

"We aren't trying to be overbearing but we were brought here to protect you and your kind. You are our responsibility. Not only that, but Medea is looking for Lela not you. We cannot chance her coming in contact with any of the Soluzari."

"I understand but we cannot stand by and let someone get hurt without helping. It is just not within our nature."

"If anyone breaches the portal, your help will be welcome but anything on the other side of the portal is our business. Nothing personal. Just the way it has to be." Jona looked up at Max who was leaning against the wall with Keith and Mikah.

Max stepped away from the wall, "I have to agree with Jona, Adinosa. But we welcome your input for our current situation. I recommend you confer with Lela so she can give you more information about Medea and her capabilities."

I led the three Soluzari from the living room and into the dining room where Lela sat. She was keeping an eye on Medea's location while talking with her friend Michael, who came to offer moral support while I had been out.

Lela was looking at me. "This is all my fault. I should have been more careful once we escaped the Underworld. Our escape was just too easy so I should have known something was up. Now, more people could be in danger of getting hurt because of me."

I could sense Lela's guilt and tried to calm her telepathically. *"This is not on you. All of this is on our parents. Their greed is what brought Medea into our lives."* Lela just nodded her head and sighed.

"Lela, I would like for you to meet some of the Soluzari. This is Adinosa who heads up the Soluzari defense including Tomas and his brother, Frech. I need you to focus and give them the run down on Medea including her strengths and weaknesses."

Lela stood up and smiled. "It is a pleasure to finally meet you. I had planned to join Aubrey on her next trip to the mountain but this came up. Please have a seat and I will tell you all I know about Medea from my time as her captive and as one of her sources of power." Adinosa and the brothers refused the chairs but moved closer to the table in order to look at the map more closely as Lela proceeded to dole out information regarding Medea and her powers.

After much discussion, we finally reached an agreement to get Medea and her minions further away from the portal entrance. Max created a sighting of Lela and me in northern Spain and let the word spread to Medea. As we watched the picture unfold before us above the dining room table, it did not take long for the word to get to Medea. She quickly relocated to the coast of Spain where the sighting had occurred. In the meantime, Max contacted the Overseers to let them know what was going on. The Overseers immediately took action by contacting local witches and warlocks to join us in northern Spain.

When Medea could not find Lela, Medea quickly became confused and frustrated as we were nowhere to be found. What Medea did find was a wall of witches and warlocks. Not only did the group from Fatimia appear but also many of the local witches and warlocks showed up from Spain, England and as far north as Ireland as a favor to the Overseers. The Soluzari remained in Fatimia. Word had quickly spread of the Underworld amoeba, Medea, to the paranormal community across many countries and how this threat needed to be nipped in the bud. She had been subtle in the past but was gathering more soldiers from the Underworld to join her in this undertaking to acquire more power. If she became too powerful, there could be no stopping her.

Once through the portal, our little group transported to join the others in Spain. I stood back behind Max with the girls, loaded with small vials of potions in a belt I created to hold them. As the others surrounded Medea and her minions, I quietly started dribbling a potion to block any outside magic from coming to her rescue. Max kept me hidden from everyone including Medea so I could complete the circle.

Medea was not startled by any means until she tried to pull in others to help her. Her eyes got wide. "I have no issues with the lot of you. Why do you stand against me? I have done nothing wrong."

Finishing the circle, I couldn't keep quiet. "That is where you're wrong, Medea. You took my sister and submitted her into slavery only to acquire more power."

"Gutsy little Empath." Medea smiled. "I bought her fair and square in a deal made many years ago."

Max stepped in, "You know that slavery of the humans, paranormal or not, is not looked kindly upon. You will refrain from this practice at once."

"I will do as I please. Who are you to tell me what I can and cannot do?"

"I am a sorcerer for the Overseers and you know Hades has an agreement with them."

"Hades does not care for you humans and would not enter into an agreement like that. We, in the Underworld, know this is just rumor."

Medea lifted her arm to throw the first blast. Max blocked it with a fire ball. He held up his hand to signal others to move. Sushi and Sasha stayed at my side as I backed away from the conflict to hide outside the circle. I was safer on the outside than on the inside.

Lela stepped forward. "This will only end in your death Medea. The choice is yours for the moment."

Medea laughed. "You may think you have the advantage here but I have a surprise for you."

A rumbling sound began and the ground began to vibrate. There was nothing we could do since it was not Medea's doing. As the sound got louder, we could see in the distance hordes of creatures coming at full speed. Our entourage began sending blasts to obliterate them. Nothing happened. Max stepped into the mix and whispered a spell that encircled our group. He then sent a blast of power at Medea. He caught her off guard and sent her flying into her minions. They all got up and immediately retaliated with their own source of energy. The barrier that I had created gave way and we were all exposed. The beasts pushed through my circle and suddenly I was transported to the entry to the portal.

Once the girls and I walked through, I was greeted by Adinosa and Frech. They were on high alert and there were several more standing not far from them. I stepped forward only to be followed by Medea. I sensed she was there alone which was a good thing.

I turned to Adinosa and Frech and yelled "EVIL!" and fell to the ground. I knew they would understand what I meant.

Adinosa and Frech sent a wave of power which Medea tried to fight off but sent her to the ground. Medea had a shocked look on her face and I knew that she was preparing to throw her power back at them.

"Take her out! Do whatever you have to do to destroy her!" I yelled at the Soluzari as I tried to stand.

The ones that were there to back up Adinosa and Frech lifted their arms and threw everything they had towards Medea. I felt the heat of the power but the force of it threw me to the ground. I looked up quick enough to see Medea go up in flames. Next thing I knew, nothing was left but a pile of dust. I reached out to the portal to see if there were more coming but apparently, only Medea had followed me out of the chaos. Why she had followed me and not continued the pursuit of Lela was beyond me. I turned to the Soluzari and smiled.

"Great work. I think that is all that will come through the portal." I rose and dusted myself off. I walked out of the direct line of fire just in case. That was an awful lot of power that they used.

We waited for a few minutes and then Max appeared. "What happened?" Max said as he looked at the pile of dust.

I was happy to see him. "Medea followed me when you transported me out of the way. She saw me go through the portal and followed only to find the Soluzari. They destroyed her. I think they are safe from exposure now."

I felt some relief in Max but still a little on guard. The girls remained silent but stayed by my side to keep me safe. I also sensed high energy among the Soluzari but they all seemed to be unharmed. A good thing because I was far from ready to do any healing on them.

"What happened back there?" I asked Max.

"When I saw that your circle had been breached, I sent you back to the portal entry and we fought off the beasts. Some turned away but the ones that kept coming were destroyed. I don't know where her minions went and that is why I am still a little worried that they may have followed Medea."

"I sensed nothing on the other side of the portal except Mcdea but she was too fast. I could only tell the Soluzari to destroy her… .and they did. It didn't take much. They are very powerful."

"Now you see why they have to be protected until they can acclimate to our planet. Capturing one could mean an all-out war. You see, one is as powerful as the whole. We haven't been able to figure out how they function as a whole and as an individual but they are linked together. If you can get control of one, it is possible that you can control the entire species. **That** we can't have. It is important that they know the risks of being linked together. We have not been able to get them to understand the danger of losing one of their own to evil. They think they can prevent that from happening but I am not so sure."

"Until we can convince them otherwise, do you think the portal is safe now that Medea has passed through it? She could have informed others before she went through."

"That is a good question and we will have to remain on high alert from here on out. We also don't know if she had a chance to contact someone of their existence before she was destroyed." Maxed looked around. "Where is Tomas?"

Adinosa explained, "He stayed back with Sahara and the others. We wanted someone fast enough to defend her in case someone or something encountered them."

"That was a smart move." Max turned to me. "Do you sense anything else on the other side of the portal besides our people?"

I reached out with my mind. "There is something sniffing around but it does not seem to be interested in the portal. It's as if it is following Medea's scent."

"I better go back through and destroy it just in case." Max was gone in a split second.

We waited to see what, if any, thing might come through besides Max but minutes later, it was Max, Jona, and a few of the others that belonged on the island.

Jona was the first to speak. "We destroyed everything that came at us. A few were injured and they are being tended to by Rigada."

"I didn't even see Rigada in the mix. When did she arrive at the site?"

Max quickly replied. "She was hidden just in case we needed her when it was all over. Once everyone returns to Fatimia, we will go on high alert and lock down. I will put a spell on the portal entrance on both sides. Jona, can you get word out to the rest of the islanders that there will be no exiting the island for the next few weeks to make sure we are secure?"

"I will do that now. I know a few shifters were out getting some supplies but I will notify them as well to get back immediately. I will let you know once everyone has been accounted for."

At that moment, Lela came through the portal a bit flustered. Others began to follow until all from Fatimia that had been at the conflict had finally come through. Lela was a little out of breath but no worse for wear. "Well, that was interesting. I don't know how those beasts knew to come for us but my guess is that Medea had made arrangements prior to her arrival at our location."

"Is everyone okay?" I asked.

Rigada answered for Lela. "I took care of the few injuries and everyone has returned to their respective homes. Nothing that I couldn't handle."

"That is good to know. Can you come with me to follow up with the Soluzari. They had a bit of a confrontation with Medea and I want to make sure that there were no issues that I can't handle."

We approached Adinosa and her crew. "Do you mind if I double check for any injuries?"

"Please feel free."

I opened my mind and sense for any negative energy. I sensed a lot of tension but no pain. I knew what pain felt like. I had a lot of experience in that as a child.

I turned to Adinosa. "All is well as far as I can tell. Thank you for letting me check. Max wouldn't forgive me if I let something get by me." I smiled.

Adinosa smiled in return and nodded her head. "We are grateful that you are concerned for our well-being."

As Max grumbled out orders to those that had gathered at the portal, he recommended that the Soluzari return to the mountain. "Can I escort you back home?" Max said to me.

"Sure, is there anything else I can do?"

"Can you keep your feelers out to sense of any unnatural beasts from home? I would rather have you there than this close to the portal. But you can be our early warning system, can't you? You can sense evil from long distances."

"Yes, I will be able to sense anything closing in on the portal that shouldn't be there. If there is evil about, I will know." I was sure if I kept my mind open and directed it in the direction of the portal, it would come up on my radar. A trailer potion would definitely help.

Once I got back to our house, I whipped up a trailer potion and headed back to the portal. With Max's permission, I stepped through and poured my detection potion around the portal entrance and then stepped back through the portal. Now, I was sure that nothing would get by my senses. I let Max know and then we waited.

C H A P T E R  13

## THE AFTERMATH

**M**AX WOULD COME AND GO, TAKING ME OUT FOR dinner on occasions. He spent most of his time on the mountain top in his home. I'm sure he was able to get the bigger picture from there. I stayed put at home waiting to sense something from the other side. I had a potion on the table that was linked to the potion around the portal. If it started to boil, things were not good. So, I sat and watched a brown potion not boil. I knew I didn't have to sit there but I couldn't get my mind off anything else. So, I sat and mindlessly worked on a jigsaw puzzle when I was not with the Soluzari, which was most of the time. Sasha and Sushi spent as much time with the Soluzari as they could and still kept an eye out for me. I was glad that Medea was dead but felt it my fault that the Soluzari had been exposed, if only temporarily. I hoped that Medea had not had the chance to get word out about them.

After a couple of weeks, Max stopped by and said we were going to remain on high alert and I was to keep my mental line open. I was fortunate enough to be able to direct my senses in that direction and continue to work on my knowledge of the new species.

I worked with Sahara and her group closely, especially Hajara, their medicinal specialist. Hajara had some experience diagnosing illnesses within their kind when they occurred. I learned much about the physical workings of the Soluzari. I was allowed to run my hands over Hajara's body to get a sense of what they felt like inside. If I closed my eyes and really concentrated, I could actually see her internal organs. I leaned too hard on her leg and felt her pain. She was very patient with me, allowing me to poke at areas that I sensed were delicate. It amazed me that someone so small, delicate, and gentle could have so much power.

Hajara had long blond hair and her nose was flatter than others. For her kind, she was not, by any means, a bad looking specimen. Her thin legs and arms were almost opal like, a mixture of colors. Hajara had a softer voice and many times I had to ask her to speak up.

When I was working with the Soluzari, Sushi and Sasha would spend much of their time with Sahara and her historian, Dinata. They were trying to get a timeline of when their family tree reached earth and began to decline. Of course, the girls would always return home with me.

Unlike humankind, the Soluzari did not dress to impress and their variety was minimal. Most of them wore something similar to a large man's dress shirt with nothing else. They felt anything else was binding. Some wore nothing at all. This was natural for them and so unlike the uptight human beings, paranormal or not.

Life kind of fell into a routine after a while. My tracking potion became a permanent centerpiece on our dining room table. I did not let my guard down at the portal since that was the only way in and out of Fatimia. I finally was formally invited to the castle on top of the mountain. Max and I spent a lot of time getting to know one another. I learned that he had not requested a position with the Overseers but was promoted to his position on the island. After years of study and travel, he had settled in at a local university when he was requested to attend a meeting of the minds, so to speak. His input was so unexpected that the Overseers' counsel decided to bring him on full time as he added a fresh new perspective to the table. Max didn't give me any details of the focus of the discussion with the Overseers as it was confidential. There were a lot of things he couldn't tell me but he shared as much as he could.

I, on the other hand, had been an open book that already had been read by Max. He had been following me for years long after he had worked with my grandmother. It was strange that all those years at the University and he never introduced himself. He had been the one to convince the Overseers to bring me on when the Soluzari arrived in our universe. Of course, my grandmother's reputation made me an easy sell.

It turned out that Max and I became friends other than a romantic couple, at least that was my perspective. I was not sure how he felt about me but we got along well. Lela became seriously involved in Michael and I saw little of her between teaching the young witches and staying with him. The girls and I were learning so much of the Soluzari as a whole and individually. We were still trying to explain how the capture of one could take down the whole if they had no way to separate. I don't think they were able to block like I could. They were powerful but had flaws. We could only wait and see.